Bound By Blood

Book Two of *The Seven Wars*

E. H. Kindred

A Novel Of The Somadàrsath

ISBN-13: 978-0985753016 (Sun Hawk Press)
ISBN-10: 0985753013

Published by Sun Hawk Press.

Typeset in: Crimson
Drop Caps in: Preciosa
Display text in: Metamorphous

The Seven Wars Series

The Immortal

Bound By Blood

Through Death Or Through Darkness

The Mirror of Dùmsaro

The Court Of The Hydra King

Time's Shadows

Storms Westward

Is it wonderful that I should be immortal? as everyone is
immortal;
I know it is wonderful, but my eyesight is equally
wonderful,
and how I was conceived in my mother's womb is equally
wonderful,
And pass'd from a babe in the creeping trance of a couple of
summers and winters to articulate and walk— all this is
equally wonderful.
And that my soul embraces you this hour, and we affect
each other
without ever seeing each other, and never perhaps to see
each other, is every bit as wonderful.

—Walt Whitman
Excerpted from "Who Learns My Lesson Complete"

Chapter One

Salazar chose to take up a post in the stable. He enjoyed being around the horses, and there were enough stablehands at work this time of day that there was always someone around. If Sorain wanted to see him, he would have to find him here, where there were plenty of people to see. Salazar hoped the presence of so many other eyes would protect him.

Not wanting to just loiter, Salazar brushed his buckskin mare, Auryn, taking his time. He worked every tangle out of her mane and tail, picked the dirt from her hooves and around the shoes, but still Sorain did not appear. The boy decided to stay a while longer, unwilling to leave the perceived safety of the stable, and so led Auryn back into her stall and tethered his father's horse out in the wide corridor among the stalls. Theramancer didn't complain (so long as Salazar brought the feed bucket with him), and stood still for the boy to brush him.

The stallion's ebony coat willingly shined under the brush and Salazar found his mind wandering as he worked. His shoulders twinged as he stretched to reach the horse's back, the bruises not quite healed from the beating Sorain had given him yesterday. That had been the final straw. When Salazar found himself cowering in the mud, looking up at his attacker from the stream behind his house, something had snapped and the boy was unwilling to take anymore. If Sorain wanted to blackmail his way back into power, he would just have to find someone else to target.

Salazar worked his way down the stallion's tall form, combing out the tangles in the long feathering at his ankles. Theramancer stamped a huge foot.

"Easy there," said the boy, patting the horse's side.

Theramancer had drawn his head out of the feed bucket and Salazar soon saw that he had not been the source of the horse's angry stomp.

Sorain had sidled into the stable, seeming at ease, and to Salazar's dismay the only stablehand left inside wandered out, leaving him alone with the captain of the guard. Sorain stalked in closer, looking at the stallion's proud head.

"Such a magnificent animal," he remarked, extending a hand toward the horse's head.

Theramancer's ears flattened and he snapped his

teeth at the captain's fingers, but Sorain had quick enough reflexes to avoid being nipped. He gave the horse an indignant look, but continued around him toward Salazar.

"What's the matter?" asked the boy. "Too afraid to hit *him* if he doesn't cooperate?"

"You wouldn't be getting rebellious with me, would you, boy?" asked Sorain, getting between Salazar and the horse.

"Call it what you like, but I've had enough," he replied. "If you think hurting and threatening me is going to be enough to manipulate my father into giving up his place here, then you are a fool."

Sorain loomed over him, pushing him back toward the opposite wall.

"Do I need to remind you what is at stake here?" Sorain growled. "I know where to find your kind and I know how to kill you. Perhaps I should send a note to your father to tell him so, after I've taken you there and have my knife poised at your throat. Something tells me he'd be quick get his nose out of my family's business then."

"Try it," Salazar snapped back, "Just see if you can get me out of this castle. See if you can even get me out of this stable—"

He saw light explode in his vision as Sorain backhanded him. Theramancer let out a shrill nicker. The boy staggered, feeling around behind him for anything he could use. He could hear Sorain's heavy footfalls closing in and the sound of his own panicked heart fluttering in his ears. His hand closed around the shaft of something and just as Sorain was lunging after him, Salazar spun, whipping the shovel up.

There was a sickening crack and Sorain's charge was brought to an abrupt halt. The captain crumpled to the dusty floor, face down, and Salazar looked down in shock and horror as the dark pool of blood grew around his head. There was a shout from the entrance of the stable and Salazar realized how it would look; he stood over the fallen, bloody body of Sorain, still clutching the shovel, the blade of which was now smeared with blood and a few pieces of hair. The boy flung the shovel away, horrified.

Salazar felt a rough pair of hands grab him by the shoulders, twisting his arms back behind him. The other stablehand had knelt beside the fallen captain, and pulled him over onto his back.

"Dead," the man growled.

Salazar felt his stomach clench as if someone had kicked him. Suddenly, his mouth was dry and his tongue felt too swollen to form a word to defend himself. He felt one of the men give him a shove and he was marched out of the stable and into the castle keep. For a moment, the boy thought they were headed for his father's study, but the men pushed him on past the door. Salazar wanted to scream, make any kind of sound to draw his father's attention, but it was as if his voice had died on the floor with Sorain. The men stopped before another door, where two guards stood.

"Tell Prince Katillis," said one of the stablehands, "This boy has killed Captain Sorain, struck him down with a shovel."

One of the soldiers stepped inside and a moment later opened the door, allowing Salazar to be shoved through to stand in the wide room in front of the desk there.

Prince Katillis was not an unkind man. For several years, he had been acting with the king's power as King Tephanis was growing old and no longer had the energy to run the castle. Salazar remembered Katillis as a warm young man, who had always smiled when they met each other in the castle, but now the prince looked like a stranger, so furrowed was his brow, so outraged were his eyes.

"Well, boy?" he asked. "Have you killed my captain of the guard?"

Salazar stood there, feeling as though he were naked. He was aware of the coldness of the stone under his feet, permeating up through his shoes, of four pairs of eyes that pierced into him, looking down at him. He felt small and helpless and suddenly wished he had never tried to handle Sorain on his own. If only he had told his mother when she'd asked him what was wrong. If only he had told his father the truth. He was aware of how alone he was in that moment, standing trapped in the room before his judge, not a soul in the world there to protect him, and it was all his fault.

"Well?" demanded the prince.

"It's true," Salazar whispered, finding a small scrap of his voice.

Katillis's face darkened even further and he turned his eyes away from the boy, a simple flick of the gaze that was laden with disappointment and disgust.

"Take him to the dungeon," he said to the guards.

Salazar felt another pair of hands fasten onto his shoulders and haul him out of the room, shoving him back down the hallway. Salazar steadied his breath enough to summon his voice back as they passed the familiar door on the right.

"Adar," he choked. Then at last, his voice freed itself into a desperate cry of, "ADAR!"

"Quiet, you!" snapped one of the guards, shoving him along the hall and down the steps.

Salazar heard the sound of a door open and Lask appeared at the balustrade, leaning over the rail. He caught sight of the guards descending the stairs below.

"What is the meaning of this?" he demanded, his snowy white face drawing into a fierce scowl at the sight.

Salazar looked up at him, and Lask was shocked at the terrified desperation in his son's face. He had never seen the boy look so distraught.

"The prince's orders," said one of the guards, not slowing down, shoving Salazar around the corner and over toward the dungeon steps.

"Stand fast!" Lask snapped, sweeping down the stairs, cloak billowing behind him with the wind of his movement, like a dark thunderhead rising behind the soldiers. Before he could catch up to them, a voice from above said,

"Lask."

He looked up to see Katillis there at the rail.

"I demand to know the meaning of this," Lask snarled, pointing to where the guards were disappearing into the dungeon with his son.

The prince strode down the steps, far slower than Lask had, and came to stand before him with a hardened expression, but one that cracked with remorse as he said,

"I am sorry, my friend. Your son has killed Captain Sorain."

Lask's rage-masked face dropped instantly into an expression of surprise. Gathering his wits, he said,

"You are certain?"

"Two of the stablehands saw it. They say the boy struck him down with a shovel."

Lask looked toward the dark stairs of the dungeon, not knowing what to think.

"This is murder," the prince continued, "I have no choice but to imprison him, regardless of his parentage—"

"You will not keep him there," Lask growled.

"Justice must be served—"

"Then serve it quickly. Summon your council. This matter will be addressed first thing in the morning!"

Katillis gave him a look of subdued indignation, looking up at him with narrowed eyes, unaccustomed to being given orders. Knowing what the prince was thinking, but not caring in the least, Lask stood all the straighter above him, scarlet eyes sparking with rage, and growled,

"I abide by your laws because I am in your kingdom, but do not forget that you are not *my* king. Let your system of justice work, but do it swiftly. I will not stand for my son to be locked down there in the dark for any more than a day. I *will* be present at his trial tomorrow and I shall not allow you nor any mortal hand to do him harm."

Katillis watched him, insulted, but found he did not have the heart to challenge the fierce immortal that loomed before him. Though not a lord of Letiana, Lask still blazed with all the commanding fire of power, a leashed inferno that would stand no disobedience.

"Very well," the prince said. "We shall conduct his trial at the ninth hour tomorrow."

Chapter Two

Three Weeks Prior

Salazar had been copying reports for his father as punishment all morning. Lask had been trying to work, but Salazar was in the mood for an argument, so the two had been bickering about Salazar's distance from Etheria. The boy had never been there, despite his protests, and he was beginning to wonder if the place existed at all. Lask gave him a message to take to Captain Astikin in the barracks (Salazar thought his father just wanted to be rid of him for a few minutes), so the boy trudged off to deliver it. As he was on his way out of the barracks, he felt the dark figure of Sorain gaining on him. All of a sudden, Salazar felt two heavy hands grab him by the shoulders and haul him over into one of the side rooms.

"Hey!" Salazar yelped.

Sorain gave him a shove over into the corner, then turned back. Salazar heard him bolt the door. The captain turned back to him and Salazar stood straight, unafraid of the man.

"What do you want?" he demanded of the captain.

"We need to have a discussion, Salazar," Sorain replied, stepping in closer. "Why don't you have a seat?" He shoved the boy down into the chair there. "Your father holds a very respectable position, you know," he said, "One of the closest advisors to the king, commander of the army. That power once belonged to *my* family and it was convenient luck that your father managed to take it from us. My father was old, and I too young to take it up myself. The king thought it fitting to appoint Lask as the replacement. I was not particularly concerned, as it was said to be only temporary and yet, here I remain, a lowly captain, some fourteen years later. I have been usurped by a ghastly foreigner."

"And how is this *my* problem?" Salazar retorted.

Without warning, Sorain whirled and backhanded the boy across the face. Salazar drew back in the chair, raising a hand to his stinging cheek, shocked.

"It is your problem," Sorain growled, grabbing the armrests of the chair to lean over the boy, "Because *you're* the one who's going to do something about it."

Salazar glared up at him, silent.

"I have heard talk," Sorain continued, withdrawing to pace back and forth across the room, "That your father will be here for some time yet. Even more concerning, I have heard that when he does at last return to his own wretched kingdom, he may leave *you* here in his stead."

Salazar had heard no such talk and wondered where Sorain was getting his information.

"And that won't do," the captain said. "I have put up with my station these long years, but I will not live out my entire life denied what is rightfully mine. That is why you will tell your father you will never take his place and you will convince him to return to his own damned kingdom and not concern himself with a land he has no right to."

"I've been trying to get him to take me to Etheria for years," Salazar growled back, "With no luck. Why do you think he'd ever listen to me now?"

"Because you can either make the leverage yourself or become it," the captain snarled back. "I'll tell you this, boy: I've been watching and listening these past years. I know where your father goes every few months. I know where to find your kingdom, and what's more, I know how to kill you."

Salazar sat in silence, watching the man with dangerous eyes. Sorain looked him over, then continued,

"Your father spends a good deal of his day here at the castle, and that leaves you and your mother alone in your house. I imagine if I bring ten men with me, I could capture the both of you and haul you off before your father would even realize it. I don't need two hostages. I'd kill that traitorous mother of yours the first chance I got. She deserves it for throwing in her lot with the likes of your father, for turning on her own kind and becoming one of *you.*"

He grabbed a handful of the boy's dark hair and hauled him up, landing him a swift punch in the ribs. Salazar doubled over, giving the perfect angle for Sorain to knee him in the gut. The boy collapsed out onto the floor with a gasp, the wind having been knocked out of him, but Sorain didn't relent, kicking his tough booted foot at his head.

Gathering his wits, Salazar grabbed him by the leg, yanking him forward and off balance, rolling over to fling himself onto the captain. The two grappled with each other, knocking the chair over in their frenzy. Salazar's father had taught him well, for the boy landed several well-placed blows on his attacker, but Sorain had the advantage of size and strength, and it wasn't long before he had wrenched the boy off of him, grabbing him by the throat and slamming him down on the floor. Salazar saw a bright flash of light as his head hit the stone and he felt Sorain pressing him down against the floor. The boy gasped, struggling for breath under the fierce grip around his neck and looked up at the captain looming over him.

"Try that again, boy, and I will put that Immortality of *yours* to the test," Sorain snarled. "And if you should even *think* of going to your father about this, I will lead my men after your mother at dawn. You can be a man and handle this quietly or I'll make you the victim of it. It's up to you."

He let go and Salazar gasped, lying sprawled on the stone, black spots still swimming in his vision from the blow to his head. Sorain marched over, unbolted the door, and was gone, flown like some sinister bat. Salazar rolled himself over, planting his palms against the cold dusty stone, pushing himself up to his hands and knees, entire body aching. He stayed there for a moment, catching his breath, letting his head clear.

No one had ever laid a hand on him or spoken to him like that in his life. Sure, his mother might give him a swift smack on the backside when he deserved it, but no one had ever truly hurt him. More than that, Salazar had never been threatened. He couldn't decide what to do. He could tell his father about what had happened and Lask would have Sorain imprisoned within the hour, but the boy imagined the captain had other contacts he could use to carry out his threats, or being the captain of the guard, he might be able to simply free himself.

Perhaps it would be best to remain silent. Sorain could only hurt him so much; no matter how hard he swung, he probably couldn't do any lasting damage. Salazar had never given much thought to the Immortality he had inherited from his father, but now he found himself grateful. It would be the magic that would allow him to take the captain's ire, protect his mother and not cause his father any trouble. After all, if Sorain knew the location of Etheria, then Salazar would have to be very careful.

Chapter Three

Salazar sank into the corner of the cell, barely able to see in the darkness. The guards had shoved him inside, and the only light that filtered in through the narrow barred window was from a single sputtering torch at the base of the stairs. The boy pulled his knees up to his chest, sitting there on the hard, cold floor. His breath shook, the only sound in the tiny cell, and he felt the weight of the darkness pressing in on him.

Just then, he heard a familiar, though now sharpened voice snap from the top of the stairs,

"Give me the keys."

The light brightened and came nearer. Salazar got to his feet and drifted toward it like a moth. His father's face appeared on the other side of the bars.

"Adar," Salazar said, so glad to see him. His voice gave way then, the tears at last breaking free at the sight of him.

Lask let himself into the cell and just managed to drop the torch into one of the iron rings set into the wall before Salazar flung himself forward. Lask caught him, enveloping the boy in the folds of his cloak, clutching him tight to his strong chest.

"Salazar," he said, "What in the world, child?"

"I'm sorry, Adar," Salazar wept, fingers twisting in the black fabric of his father's shirt.

"So it is true then?" Lask felt the boy nod against him. He rubbed a hand along the shaking back under his fingers with a sigh. "Why?"

"He hurt me," Salazar murmured, "Several times. He's been doing it for weeks. He wanted to use me to get to you. He told me not to say anything. He threatened me and told me he would hurt Mother. He said I needed to find a way to make you give up your position here, or else he'd kidnap us. He knew where the Gate was, Adar. He said he knew how to kill us and that he would kill her."

"Why didn't you say anything, my son?" Lask asked, knowing now why Salazar had been so out of sorts in the past weeks. "I could have stopped this the moment it started."

"I'm sorry," the boy whispered. He ran his thumb over the embroidered gold vines that ran along the seam of his father's shirt, wanting to escape into their twining coils. "I was scared. I thought I could make him stop if I just showed him I wasn't afraid of him anymore. He hit me again, and I was afraid he was going to kidnap me, so I just grabbed whatever was closest to defend myself— I wasn't thinking. I didn't mean to, I just... when he came after me, it just happened..."

Lask ran a hand over the boy's dark hair, feeling him shaking under his touch.

"What are they going to do to me?" Salazar asked.

"I don't know," Lask confessed. He reached down and dislodged Salazar's face from his chest, cupping a hand under the boy's chin so those green eyes looked up at him. "But I promise you, I will not let them hurt you and I will not let them keep you down here in the dark." He studied the shaken, terrified, horror in the young face he held. "Understand?"

Salazar sniffed and nodded. Lask held his head against his chest again until he felt the boy settle under his touch.

"Katillis will not let me take you home," he said, "And I must tell your mother. I will make sure that you are sent a good supper tonight and a blanket so you don't get cold. I will be back as soon as the sun rises." He bent down and kissed the boy's head, feeling Salazar's reluctant fingers let go of him.

Chapter Four

When Lask arrived back at their house, he led Theramancer into the stable. He was so festering with a swarm of emotions, he could hardly focus long enough to pull off the horse's tack. When he went inside, Myranda met him there at the door.

"What's wrong?" she said, knowing just by his face and agitated gait. "Where is Salazar?"

"In the dungeon of the Letian castle."

"What? Why? You *left* him there?" Myranda exclaimed.

"I had little choice," Lask replied, a growling edge on his voice. "He has killed the captain of the guard. Two people saw him bash the man's head in with a shovel and he admits to it."

Myranda was aghast.

"*Why?*" she breathed.

Lask explained everything Salazar had told him, bristling at the thought of what had been done to his son.

"Our poor boy," Myranda murmured, stunned, "Why didn't he tell us? Now what will—?"

"I have arranged for his trial to be in the morning," Lask said. "I will see they do not harm him or keep him imprisoned." He moved around her, sliding his sword off from over his shoulder. "Damn it all," he snarled, hanging it on the back of one of the chairs at the table. "This would never have happened in Etheria. No soldier of mine would dare to touch him and if they did, *they* would be the ones in the dungeon. *Ignorant, insolent, mortals*!" His long fingers clutched the back of the chair as if it were someone's neck.

Myranda chanced shifting nearer to him, laying a hand on his back.

"Had we been *there*, he would be but a babe," Lask growled over his shoulder at her. "By the time he was a young man I would have known him well enough to know what was happening, not have been left guessing until it was too late. Damn this dying, hurried country!" He swept away from her, crossing the room to lean instead upon the counter, looking out the window there. His shoulders fell like the tide with the heavy breath that rushed out of him. "Salazar looks so much like my brother at that age," he muttered, almost as if to himself, "Apparently he has the same accursed knack for accidental murder." He ran a hand through his hair.

Myranda went over and wrapped her arms around him, leaning her head against his back. Lask put a hand over hers, turning to face her and drawing her into his arms.

"I'm sorry, my dear," he murmured into her bright hair, knowing he should not be snapping so when she was as distressed as he was. He held her there against him, feeling her lean her head against his chest. "I will do what I can for him."

Chapter Five

Salazar was grateful his father had left the torch in his cell. Its flickering light helped the darkness to not feel so heavy. He sat there with his back against the wall, staring ahead at the door, his horror and fear congealed into a stunned daze. He did not know how much time passed, but later he saw a shadow out in the hallway and a familiar soldier appeared.

It was Sifkin, a man who had served under his father during the war with Galator, and who had since become one of his father's most favored mortals.

"Sorry to see you down here, Salazar," said the soldier. "But here," he set something down on the floor and fiddled with the lock so he could come in, "Brought you some supper."

He offered out a large bowl of stew, steaming with a hearty smell that reminded the boy just how hungry he was. Salazar took it with a frail, but grateful, smile.

"Thank you," he said.

"Of course, young sir," answered the solider, passing him a large biscuit. "Also brought you this." He laid a large, thick blanket out on the floor. "It's no feather bed, but it should keep you warm and help the stone not hurt so."

"Thank you," murmured the boy again.

"Ah, cheer up, lad," said Sifkin, clapping him on the shoulder. "So you accidentally rid the world of one of its many asses. There are worse things a man can do. Don't you fret; your father is a fine man. No matter what they do tomorrow, he'll see that you're looked after."

Chapter Six
One Week Prior

"I'm worried about him," said Myranda as she brushed the tangles out of her hair, unaware that their son was eavesdropping just beyond their bedroom door.

Lask looked at her over the top of his book from his place leaned back against the headboard.

"He's been so tight-lipped lately," Myranda was continuing, "He's normally so talkative when it's just us. He's been thinking about something, but won't say what it is."

"He has seemed distracted of late," Lask agreed.

"And he's hurt himself so often these past few weeks; telling you he fell down the castle steps, then slipping down the embankment in the creek. It's not like him to be so clumsy."

"I'm wondering if he got into a fight," Lask replied, "His knuckles were scraped and he was careful with his breath, like someone had kicked him."

"Maybe he slipped into the kitchens to visit Leum and the two had a scrap."

"Leum is a scrawny little thing. I don't think he'd stand a chance if Salazar took a notion to hit him."

Myranda couldn't argue, asking instead,

"If he did, why wouldn't he say anything? He's hardly ever lied to us; he knows better. He's normally not very good at keeping quiet about things that are bothering him." She came over to slide under the blankets beside him. "He told me today that he can take care of whatever it is on his own."

"And perhaps he can. He's very smart and I've no doubt he could take care of himself if he had to."

"I know, but still," Myranda grumbled. She turned her head to rest against his shoulder. "I worry about him. I wonder why he thinks he can't tell us things anymore. Could be his age, I suppose, though he's normally got a bit more sense than most of them."

Lask pulled the ribbon bookmark down between the pages again and set the book aside, raising his arm for her to slide under. He ran a hand over her shoulder, saying,

"I worry about him as well. He's grown so much, so fast. I feel as though I've had no time at all with him. Had we stayed in Etheria, he would not look that age for another three hundred years."

"As much as I like our son, I *am* glad he wasn't a

squalling baby for a hundred years," said Myranda.

Lask chuckled. Myranda tilted her head up, seeing the sad sort of smile that had settled over his pale face.

"Are you sorry you were persuaded to stay here?" she asked him, voice quiet.

"Sometimes," Lask confessed. "I stayed at the behest of Lavancer and Tephanis, as well as you. While my presence here and the correspondence with Etheria have done much good for the mortal kingdoms, I am sorry that our son has grown so quickly."

Myranda stroked a hand over his chest. As a former mortal, she could not yet imagine the slow aging rate of the Immortals, and so thought very little about Salazar's growth. Lask, on the other hand, could see the changes in the boy with every passing day, and she could tell at times it weighed heavily on him.

"Sometimes I don't think he likes me very much," Lask murmured. "And I think part of him hates me for keeping him away from Etheria."

"It's for the best," said Myranda. "You said yourself there have been rumors Vortearigan has been seen. If we stayed in Etheria, if Salazar stayed little for that long, he would be a prime target."

"I know. Yet I know too that land is in his blood, ties that cannot be fathomed by the mind, but only felt in the soul. Being parted from it brings an ache in the heart.

Though he has never set foot there, I know Salazar feels it as I do, and I cannot imagine the kind of frustration it must cause him... and it pains me to know that I am the cause of that."

Myranda kissed his shoulder, wrapping an arm around his waist.

"Salazar loves you," she told him, "And he's so much like both of us, so much like you. I can see you in his face when he looks at me, especially that devilish little grin he gets sometimes. One day I think he'll understand why we chose what we did for his childhood."

Out in the hallway, Salazar stepped back from the door, tiptoeing away down the hall. He had heard his parents speaking as they went into their room for the night, and having heard his name, he crept out to eavesdrop, unable to resist the temptation.

His father's words saddened him. Salazar did not hate his father by any stretch of the term. Certainly there was some resentment in him from being kept in the dark about Etheria, but the boy found his father's stories fascinating and deep down, he quite admired his father. Even if Salazar made himself onerous at times, he would never want to cause either of his parents any lasting pain.

The boy settled back into his bed, wondering if he ought to confess his interactions with Sorain. He decided against it, as he had done earlier, deciding it was high time he started taking care of himself, and from the sounds of it, his father did not need anything else to deal with at the moment. Salazar thought himself to be quite capable for someone of his age; he just needed a plan and somewhere safe he could confront Sorain.

Chapter Seven

Salazar slept only fitfully that night, drifting in and out of a tired, worry-filled slumber. It was cold in the cell, but the blanket Sifkin had brought him kept him from getting chilled. It was more the quiet and the eerie darkness of the dungeon that kept him on edge. It would have been quiet in his own room, but it was of a different sort; he could always hear the hushed sound of the trees outside, the occasional creaks of the floorboards when his father rose to rekindle the fire late in the night. Here there was only deadened, empty silence.

When morning came, Lask kept his promise. He appeared there at the cell door at dawn, bringing the boy some breakfast and clean clothes. The two sat in the cell together, awaiting the hour of the trial, and though the boy did not know it, his father felt just as trapped as he did. When the hour came, Lask rose and led the boy out of the dungeon, up to the council hall.

They entered into a tall chamber with exposed rafters. A long table sat in the center of the room. At the far end of it sat the aged King Tephanis and his son, Prince Katillis. There were six other stone-faced men sitting there waiting. They all looked up as the pair entered.

Salazar could feel all of those eyes boring into him and his stomach clenched at the sight of them. His father's firm hand on his back steadied him, guiding him over to sit at the foot of the table. Lask settled into the chair beside him, a motion that looked more like a panther crouching to spring.

"We are here today," said Tephanis, his voice grown hoarse with age, "To serve justice for the murder of Captain Sorain, who was a devoted guard of the castle and a personal servant to me, just as his father before him had been. As I understand it, there was a reason for this murder. Can you tell us what that might be, boy?"

"Sorain threatened me several times so that I would apply leverage to my father," Salazar replied, and he was surprised at how steady his voice remained. "All of those times he inflicted physical harm on me. I never intended to kill him. It was an accident when I tried to defend myself."

"If he indeed was threatening you," said one of the counselors (Salazar recognized him as Chamberlain Razmus), "Why did you not simply come forward then?

Why not tell your father or even someone here at the castle?"

"He told me if I did, there would be dire consequences for myself and also my mother. He threatened to kidnap both of us and kill us. He claimed he knew how to do it."

"Why you?" asked another of the men at the table. "Why would Sorain concern himself with a boy?"

"He claimed my father stole power that was rightfully his. He wanted me to persuade my family to leave."

"How long did this go on?" asked Razmus.

"Over three weeks."

"And during that time, did you consider doing anything to stop him?"

"Recently I decided to stand up to him. I thought if he saw he could not frighten me anymore, he would have no choice but to stop."

"So you did plan to confront him then?" asked one of the counselors.

"Yes."

"You planned, then, to attack him if he attacked you?"

"That is hardly fair, counselor," Lask replied. "Choosing to defend oneself does not, by any stretch, equal a planned murder."

"Nonetheless," said Razmus. "The boy has killed

someone. Accident or not, it cannot simply be brushed aside."

"The penalty for murder is death," said one of the men.

"You could not kill him even if you *did* think I'd stand by and allow you," Lask snarled.

The man gave a haughty sniff at the two immortals.

"Give him a good flogging and send him on his way," said another.

"I think you misunderstand me, counselors," Lask replied. "If you believe I will stand for my son being harmed in *any* way, then you are all fools."

A deathly quiet settled over the table.

"Have him repay his debt in service," suggested one. "Make him a messenger."

"He's just a boy," scoffed another from across the table. "I wouldn't trust him to ride alone with important correspondence."

"A simple servant here in the castle then—"

"You want to leave a murderer free to wander the halls as he pleases? Accident or not, he has proven what he is capable of and is now a risk to leave free, particularly here if he should take a notion to kill again."

One of the counselors had been silent the entire session and now chose to speak but one word,

"Exile."

The counselors exchanged glances, nodding.

"Seven years of exile," said King Tephanis from the head of the table. "He should not be forever an enemy of this kingdom for a mistake in his youth." He paused and looked down the table. "We will not harm your son, Lask, though it would be our custom to do so, but for this I ask something of you. I will have your son banished from this kingdom; he will be taken deep into the Great Forest of Kwynn, far from any town or village so that he cannot further explore any murderous urges he may develop. However, I ask that *you* remain here in Letiana. My banishment of your son does not mean the banishment of you. I don't want you simply packing up your family and returning to your homeland. You have helped me conduct great work and reform in this kingdom, but work that is still precarious. I believe it is your king's wish that you stay as ambassador here between our worlds, and should you leave us now, I will take it as an abandonment of our kingdom and an act of hostility from yours."

The blaze with which Lask's gaze fell on the king seemed as though it should have cremated the old man, but Tephanis sat there under it, steady and unmoving. Lask glanced down to Salazar, who sat next to him, looking up at him with pitiable frightened eyes. How much Lask wanted to draw the boy close to his side, to keep him clutched under his arm from the mortals who would tear him away, but what choice did he have? There were several mortals who knew the location of the Gate and Tephanis could utilize them to find Etheria. If he chose to declare war on the Immortals and led an army to their homeworld, soldiers now trained by Lask's own hand, their Immortality would no longer matter. As much as it pained him, Lask the Protector could not put his love for his son above the safety of his kingdom.

"Will you settle with this, Lask?" asked the king.

"Yes," he said, and the word dug icy talons into his heart as he spoke it.

Salazar looked up at him, and Lask found that he could hardly look at those wide, heart-wrenching eyes. He put a hand on the boy's knee under the table, but Salazar shifted his leg away.

"Then it is settled," said Prince Katillis. "The boy will be escorted north to the border of the forest tomorrow morning." He nodded to the guards at the door. "Take him back to the dungeon."

"*No,*" Lask snarled. "My son shall return with me this night."

With that, he stood up from the table and swept out of the room, drawing Salazar in his wake like a leaf in the wind of a tempest, and no one dared to stop them.

Chapter Eight

The two rode out of the castle in silence, and Lask could feel Salazar watching him, but could think of nothing to say.

"Why?" asked the boy at length, and his voice was quiet (holding back a sob or a scream, Lask did not know), "Why are you letting them do this? I thought you were going to keep them from hurting me. You promised."

"They aren't hurting you," Lask replied.

"Yes they are!" Salazar exclaimed, voice breaking. "They're throwing me out into the wilderness for seven years! *Alone*! You're just going to *let* them?"

"I will make sure that you are safe," Lask told him. "I have plenty of contacts in the Great Forest—"

"The Etherians I suppose," Salazar snarled. "So *now* you'll entrust me to them. All these years, you'd never even let me *near* that Gate and now you're casting me off on them."

"I have little choice, Salazar," Lask said, voice quiet.

"You have every choice!" the boy cried. "You could be *king* of this place if you wanted. You supposedly command *thousands* of immortal soldiers. Not a soul in this world can hurt you or best you. What's to be afraid of with a few mortals? *Why* won't you fight for me?"

"I would have," Lask snarled, "But you waited until my hands were tied." He sighed and looked skyward, forcing the edge out of his voice. "There is so much at work here, my son. Etheria and Earth are more entwined now than they have ever been, and perhaps it is for the worse, but it was not my decision to make. For all my power, I must still answer to our people."

"*Your* people," growled Salazar. "And the fact that you love them more than your own son will make it so I *never* want them to be mine."

The boy dug his heels into his horse's sides, making the mare canter on ahead of Theramancer. Lask followed behind him, not showing how much the boy's words stung. When they reached the house, Salazar left his horse in the yard and went inside, storming into his room and slamming the door. When Lask entered, Myranda was there, looking down the hall where Salazar had disappeared, confused and concerned.

"He's home," she said.

"Only for a day," Lask replied. He drew her into his

arms, bowing his head to hide his face in her hair and she whispered,

"What is it?"

Chapter Nine

From inside his room, Salazar could hear the lowered voices of his parents, and then the sound of his mother crying. He stretched out on the bed, hearing her sobs, muffled, doubtless in his father's chest, and the sound of them released the tears that he had held back. He lay there on his back, staring up at the ceiling, feeling so very lost.

His parents' voices rose out in the parlor, and despite the situation, Salazar could not resist the temptation to investigate. As he sat up to go to the door, he could hear his mother saying,

"Damn their laws! No one in this house is mortal. If this is the thanks they give you for all these years you've spent here, if all the things you have sacrificed for them are not even enough to pardon our son—"

"The king must not choose favorites in the face of justice—"

"I hardly think rewarding loyal service with mercy

would be enough to undo all their work against corruption. For heaven's sake, if Tephanis is so concerned about good relations with Etheria, he's certainly not showing any goodwill, is he?"

Salazar waited, but if his father made a reply, the boy couldn't hear it.

"And I can't believe you are allowing this," Myranda growled. "Where is our Protector?"

"What would you have me do?" Lask snarled back. "I would flee this forsaken country in heartbeat if I could. There have been *many* nights I have wished to. I am but a servant in this place, here at the command of my king and our Senate—"

"Then maybe it's time you make your case to them—"

"It's too late for that. Tephanis knows too much. If we leave now, he could find the Gate if he wanted—"

"And what if he did?" Myranda demanded. "I have seen your army in action and they would make quick work of any mortal that challenged them."

"Perhaps at first, but Earth is a wide world, much bigger than Etheria. If word of the Gate's location were to spread, all hell would break loose and no amount of our valor would hold back the sheer rush of desperate mortality. I *want* to go home. I want to keep our son at our side, but *tell me,* my love, how can I do that when the fate of our world hangs by thread over my head?"

There was a pause, and Myranda's voice came again, quieter, and Salazar could not catch all of her words. The boy opened the door just a crack and caught sight of the reflection of his parents in the mirror that hung farther down the hallway. Myranda had hidden herself against Lask's chest again and Lask had his arms around her, holding onto her with a desperate strength. Salazar shut the door without a sound and went to flop out on the bed again, frustrated with both of them and everything else.

In time, the door opened and his father stepped inside. Salazar wanted so much to hate him, but when he saw him, he found he simply couldn't. Lask looked like someone had beaten him, and there was such a shadow of sorrow over his face, Salazar almost wept again at the sight of him.

Lask slipped the red leather strap off of his shoulder, taking his sword in his hands, and came to sit on the edge of the bed. He looked down at the sheathed blade.

"This sword is almost as old as our world," he said. "It came from a star that fell at your great-great-grandfather's feet. The Creator Himself instructed him how to forge it. It has been carried by four men in all that time and it has weighed so very heavy on all of our shoulders." He looked down to his son's face. "I know this is not fair; none of it is fair, nor will it ever be. We do not choose the blood in our veins, and ours binds us to the most difficult task that was ever set upon a man. I did not ask for it, and neither did you, but one day, you will bear the weight of this blade on your shoulders, for you are bound to carry it by blood and by God, just as I am, and perhaps then you will understand why I must let you go. I love you more than life itself, and I would lay down my life for you in an instant. But, my son, it would not only be *my* life laid down, and as much as I love you, I am bound to think first of my kingdom, even if it means a torture worse than death for me."

Salazar sat up then and slipped his arms around his father's neck, putting his head on that weary shoulder. Lask put an arm around the boy, hearing Salazar whisper by his ear,

"I'm sorry I yelled at you, Adar."

"You're scared," Lask replied, "We all are, but you will be safe and cared for these next seven years, that I will promise you. I just need a bit of time to decide the best way to do that. You'll just have to trust me."

Chapter Ten

When Salazar was getting ready for bed that evening, he found his mother in the room across the hall. She looked up when he entered and smiled at him, a smile so fond yet full of sorrow, Salazar found it more tragic than if she had burst into tears at the sight of him.

Myranda drew him to her, bowing her head to inhale the smell of his hair, as if memorizing it and stowing it away.

"You know I love you," she murmured, holding him against her bosom. "Try to get some sleep." She kissed his head. "Your father's in the parlor."

Salazar nodded, hearing her heart beating sadly in her chest under his ear. He pulled away from her, knowing in the morning he would have a much worse goodbye to make. He left the room and went down the hall. The boy could see the long shadow stretching out into the hallway and stopped short to peer into the parlor.

His father stood there before the fire, a tall silhouette against the lapping flames. There was a steadiness about him; he stood perfectly still, as though carved from marble, one arm resting on the mantle as he looked down into the fire. The flames cast his white skin in an orange-gold glow, reflecting in his eyes, glinting off his ring, as if he himself were ablaze.

It was in that moment Salazar found himself looking not at his father, but at an ancient and proud creature, grounded in an eternal surety and silent strength. Though he was still, Salazar could see that thoughts were swirling in his mind, that he was sorting through them, weighing each of them carefully, planning out the days ahead with as much craft and cunning as he had the plans of battle that had killed so many men.

Salazar was reluctant to disturb him, so keen and focused he seemed, but Lask sensed his son's presence and turned his head to look at him. Those scarlet eyes seemed endless, weighted with all the countless days of life, and as Salazar stood beneath their gaze he felt small in a way that he had never felt before. Gone was his father; here was the man who had slain the griffin, the one who struck fear into the hearts of brave men.

"Goodnight, Adar," Salazar whispered, as if afraid to speak too loudly.

"Goodnight, my son," replied Lask, and his voice was

quiet and gentle, summoning back the boy's father out of the shadow of the Somadar.

He stepped forward and pulled his son into his embrace, and Salazar lingered there. The boy felt small against his father's strong form and very safe. For a moment, the outside world was held at bay and he was hidden in those familiar arms.

Chapter Eleven

After Salazar had gone to bed, Lask found Myranda already in their bedroom for the night. She was sitting on the edge of the bed and he could tell she had been crying again. He sat down beside her and put an arm around her shoulders. She sniffed and looked up at him, her blue eyes entreating him to say something, *anything*, to ease the pain of losing their son.

"In the morning, after he has gone, I will ride northward," Lask said, "And enter the forest of Kwynn before he arrives. I will contact Fildahorr and arrange for Salazar to be taken into the care of the Warauls at the Gate. They will take good care of him, I am certain."

Myranda sniffed and nodded, leaning her head against his shoulder.

"We should pack some of his things tonight," Lask continued, "So I can take them with me to be waiting for him when he arrives." He rubbed a hand over her arm. "Sifkin carries letters to and from Etheria every other week. We can send things to Salazar through him, and visit him ourselves when I must go to Etheria for the Senate meetings."

Myranda nodded again, knowing he had a good plan and that Salazar would be safe at the Gate, though it did little to ease the pain.

"I just don't know what I'll do without him," she murmured, "You're at the castle most of the day; it's going to be so quiet here. Our friends are all in Etheria."

"I plan to write to Lavancer," Lask said, "And try to convince him to let us return soon. I have lost much of the patience I once had with the mortals, and I fear that keeping their world in contact with ours will only lead to trouble."

Chapter Twelve

It was a restless night for everyone in the house. Salazar could hear his parents stirring even at late hours, could hear his father pacing in the parlor late in the night. The boy himself could not bring himself to move, staring, frozen, up at the ceiling, riddled with guilt and uncertainty. He felt like a monster for having taken a life, and like a terrible son for bringing such shame and pain down upon his parents.

When morning came, Salazar trudged into the kitchen, feeling sick. His mother smiled at him, but he could see through it. He sank down across from his father.

"Here," said Myranda, pushing a tray of fruit toward him, "You should have some breakfast."

Lask unfolded a piece of parchment and slid it over so Salazar could see it.

"Your escorts will likely leave you somewhere around here," Lask told him, indicating a place on the map, "Once they have gone, I want you to make your way here," he tapped a place he had circled, "There will be someone waiting for you there. Go with them and they will make sure you are taken care of." He refolded the parchment, "Hide this in your shirt and don't let your guards see it."

Salazar obeyed, tucking it under the folds of his shirt, wondering what his father was up to. There was a knock on the door. Lask rose to answer it and Salazar could hear the voice of a soldier out in the foyer. He stood up and Myranda put an arm around his shoulders, walking with him to the front door. Once there, she drew him into her arms.

"I love you so much," she told him, then dropped her voice to whisper in his ear, "I'll write to you often and we'll see each other much sooner than *they* think we will." She drew back, looking at him and blinking back the tears, saying, "Take care of yourself, behave, and don't do anything stupid." She cupped his face in her hands and kissed his head. "It will be alright, you'll see."

Salazar nodded, though he could see that she was having a hard time convincing herself of it as well, and whispered a return, 'I love you.' He turned to stand before his father and Lask enveloped him against his tall form.

"I love you, Adar," he said, trying to keep his voice steady.

"I love you, my son," Lask replied, kissing the boy's

head, then bowed his head to say into his ear, "You will see and learn things these next few years that you have never imagined. Do not fight them, for they are part of who we are, and they will lead you to a great, wide world. You will be alright," he said, and Salazar believed it more than when Myranda had said it, "Our Creator sees even this place, and He will keep you safe. Don't be afraid, my son, for things are rarely as dark as they seem."

He looked down at the boy and though his eyes were darkened with sadness, Salazar saw the familiar, steady, fire that was always there, and it gave him a bit of comfort. He pulled back, feeling the coldness of the morning close around him where his father's arms had been.

The soldiers waited for him outside, and they motioned him toward the extra horse there. Salazar pulled himself into the saddle, trying not to let his guards see the shame and sorrow that threatened pour out of him. They set out into the trees, and Salazar looked back. His mother had lost the battle with her tears and they streamed down her face, though she made not a sound. Lask had put an arm around her, and as they disappeared from view, Salazar had never seen such a look of profound, unfathomable sorrow as what had settled over his father's face.

Chapter Thirteen

When the soldiers had disappeared, Myranda turned her head against her husband's chest, closing her eyes.

"Go," she whispered.

Lask released her, took up the bag they had packed for Salazar, and went back to the stable, where he led Theramancer out. His fingers worked through the straps of the bridle from their own memory, his mind too preoccupied to remember how to fasten the buckles. Theramancer watched him with dark eyes, sensing the sorrow in him. As he set the saddle up on the stallion's tall back, Theramancer turned his head and let out a low, rumbling neigh from deep in his throat. Lask paused.

"They've taken my son from me," he murmured to the horse, tightening the saddle girth, "And they won't let me go with him." He fastened the buckle, then put a pale hand against the stallion's face, stark against the black fur. "For all the power in my blood, I am a prisoner as much as he is."

He tied the bag on behind the saddle, then pulled himself up, turning his mount to go galloping away into the forest.

Lask took the back roads, riding through the day and into the night, borne northward by Theramancer's swift pounding hooves. He stopped only long enough for Theramancer to drink and catch his breath. He did not let himself think much, unwilling to let his thoughts linger on the dark absence of his son that he would have to endure in the coming years. He did not want to let himself think for fear that he would grow angry and bitter, both at the kings that had kept him there and at Myranda, who had persuaded him to stay far better than the kings could have, yet think he did. It was inevitable in those lonely stretches of deserted country. None of them could have known this would happen and if he had been steadfast in his desire to return to Etheria at the beginning, he would not be here now. If he had paid more attention to his son than to the wishes of the mortal king, perhaps he would have known what was happening before it went so far. In the end, Lask could only blame himself.

As the sun was coming up, Theramancer slowed in a pasture at the edge of the tree line, sides heaving, and planted his feet, casting an eye back at his rider.

"Alright," Lask conceded, exhausted himself, "We'll

rest for a while." He slid from the saddle, then unbuckled the tack. Theramancer shook his head, glad to be free of the bridle for a while and walked over to a small creek nearby, plunging his face in to drink. Lask knelt on the bank and took a drink from it as well, then sat back, taking stock of their surroundings. It was still miles to the Gate, though he guessed they would arrive there some time in the night. The mortal horses that carried Salazar and his guards were far slower than Theramancer. There was no question Lask would arrive in the Great Forest before they did, so he allowed himself to lay out on his back in the grass, folding his hands behind his head.

Having drunk his fill, Theramancer plodded over and flopped out beside him, resting his great back against his master's side. Lask rubbed a hand over the stallion's strong shoulders, fingers absently working through his mane. He drifted off to sleep for a while, dozing fitfully as the sun came up. When he awoke, it was several hours before noon. He roused Theramancer and buckled the tack back on.

He rode on through the day and entered the forest of Kwynn as the sun was going down. He pressed on, riding through the trees as the moonless night settled in with almost total darkness. He had passed this way many times, so Theramancer knew the way and carried him toward the heart of the forest. Even if neither horse nor rider could see, there was a sense that drew them on, knowing that each step brought them closer to home.

In the bitter watches of the night, as the underbrush thickened, Lask drew his horse to a halt and called out into the trees,

"Guardians!"

His voice echoed off the trees, and only the faint sighing of the wind answered him, but he knew something had heard him. Sure enough, it was not long until a voice spoke out of the darkness.

"Somadar, why have you come to us so late?"

"I must speak to Fildahorr," Lask replied, "I must ask him a very important favor."

"Of course, lord. I shall bring him to you."

The woods were silent and though Lask heard no sound of movement in the leaves, he knew the creature was gone. It was difficult to tell how much time had passed, but there later came a new voice out of the shadows,

"How may I be of service, Somadar?"

"Fildahorr," Lask said, "I need your help, my friend."

Chapter Fourteen

Salazar looked back through the trees two days later, seeing the Letian soldiers disappearing back down the road. Though they had been his captors, the boy felt a sense of despair settle over him at their departure. After all, they were the only people for many miles, perhaps the only people he would see for a long time.

He pulled the map out from under his shirt, trying to keep himself from thinking on the sheer *aloneness* of his situation. The boy set out into the trees, following the thick black line his father had drawn along the map. The way was wild, with no path that he could discern, the forest floor littered with fallen branches and brambles that snagged at his legs.

As he walked on while the sun peaked high, he caught sight of a trail in the damp dirt and leaves: horse hooves. They were large, broad tracks, bespeaking an enormous horse, with a faint wispy pattern around the edges, brushstrokes from the long hair that must have grown at the ankles. Salazar found himself thinking the tracks resembled those of his father's horse. They seemed to be going the same direction as the map was leading him.

The brush grew thicker, Salazar having to fight his way through briars and foliage, and as he did so, he got the distinct feeling of being watched. He could feel the prickling sensation of several gazes upon his back, and looked over his shoulder, but saw nothing in the woods around him. Deciding he was just being jumpy, he continued on.

A stick snapped behind him.

Salazar whirled back, but the forest was as empty as before. He looked up into the branches above him and caught a faint sound, his eyes snapping back to the ground, seeking the source, but it was silent. It had almost sounded like something was laughing at him.

He turned and set off again, quickening his pace. Though he heard no sound around him, he knew something was following him. He walked faster, his stride getting quicker and quicker, but still the silence pursued him. It wasn't long until he was weaving through the trees at a full run, leaping over fallen branches, tearing through the brush, like a deer fleeing the hounds. He came upon a small stream and stopped short, arms swinging to balance himself at the abrupt halt.

A tall, wolf-like creature stood on the bank opposite him. It was dark brown with pale yellow eyes. It had large ears, and long spikes of fur grew up from the top of its head, continuing down its neck. There was an intelligence in its canine face as it regarded him with an expression that was both curious and skeptical.

Salazar backed away, only to see two more of the creatures behind him; one was black, the other russet brown. They closed in on him, surrounding him there at the stream. The boy held up his hands, as if surrendering, murmuring in a voice weak with fear,

"Easy, wolf... things."

"*Wolf things*?" the black one exclaimed, its face contorting in indignation.

Salazar's jaw dropped and he leapt back, startled.

"Easy, boy," said the creature behind him on the opposite bank. "You're nervous as a spring rabbit."

"You can speak," Salazar said, amazed, looking over his shoulder at the creature.

"Obviously," it answered, in a voice the boy decided was masculine. "Gracious, child, has your father taught you *nothing*?"

"How do you know my father?"

"I would take that as a *no*," said the russet colored one, and Salazar decided it was a female, for her voice was higher and the spikes of fur on her head were shorter than her companions.

"Your father is a lord of Etheria," said the one behind him, "And therefore a lord of us."

"You're warauls," Salazar said, amazed.

"Oh so you *do* know us then, young sir?" remarked the black one. "And here I thought you were just an ignorant—"

"Your father instructed us to meet you here," said the dark brown one with a pointed look across the stream at his companion, "And escort you through the Tress to the Den."

"The Tress?"

The waraul gave him a skeptical look.

"The mile wide radius around the Gate," said the russet one, as if it were obvious.

"The Gate to Etheria?" asked Salazar, suddenly eager.

"Calm yourself, boy," replied the waraul on the other side, "You're not going *through* it. Your father left orders for us to take you into our care. You will be living in the Den with us. You will find some of your belongings awaiting you there. Come, Fildahorr is expecting you."

Wary, but intrigued, Salazar stepped across the stream, following the dark brown waraul away through the trees, the other two flanking him.

"I'm Blair," said the russet one, rubbing her head

against his side in greeting, "And that's my mate, Avamor."

The black one nodded from his other side.

"And I am Seppish," said the one who led them, "I am the Guardian's second in command."

"Guardian?" echoed Salazar.

"Fildahorr, Guardian of the Tress," Seppish glanced over his shoulder, "Older than the Gate itself and charged with defending it by your great-great-grandfather."

Salazar looked ahead to see an enormous wall of brush rising up before them. It was so thick he could see nothing beyond. Seppish led him along the wall until they came to an opening, where two other warauls sat on guard. They nodded to Salazar as he went by. The boy passed through after Seppish and into a large clearing. His eyes fixed onto the enormous archway at the other end. It was carved seemingly from a single piece of pale green stone. Vines twisted down either side of it, and along the top was a line of strange symbols. At the peak of the arch was a circle, divided down its center, the right half white, the left half black.

"The Gate to Etheria," Seppish said, seeing the boy gawking. "Don't get any ideas."

Salazar kept his eyes on the arch as the warauls led him through the clearing. There were others milling around and there was a circle of about ten of them sitting off to one side, where one was standing, apparently telling a story. Salazar caught a few of the words as he passed:

"—and never had there been so fierce a lion! Such snapping teeth and steely claws, eyes like fire, so proud a mane! The man thought surely he would die, but then he saw the thorn—"

Salazar passed out of earshot, following Seppish over to a stone-lined hole in the ground. At first he thought it was a well shaft, but then he realized there was a staircase there, leading down into a passageway below. Seppish trotted down and Salazar followed.

It was a long stone corridor, supported by carved pillars, looking more like it belonged in a castle than underground. A strange golden light illuminated it.

"What is that light?" asked the boy, curious.

"A spell," explained Seppish, claws clicking on the floor as he led him on, "Magic laid down by the Ancient Time."

Salazar's father had told him of the Ancients, though Salazar had never really understood them. They were apparently functions of the world, such as Time, incarnate. Salazar never liked to dwell on the idea too much, as it made his head hurt. Seppish stopped before a tall oak door and knocked a forepaw against it.

"Come in," came a voice.

Seppish nosed the door open and motioned Salazar

inside.

It was a large room, lit by the same strange light. The walls were lined in low shelves, packed with books, and several intricate metal wall hangings hung on the stone walls. There were six long pillows strewn about the floor and a potted vine growing in the corner. Lying upon one of the fluffy red pillows was another waraul. He was not the largest Salazar had seen, indeed he was a slighter figure than Seppish, but there was a strength about him that bespoke a creature not to be trifled with. His face was smooth and wise, his deep brown eyes intelligent and keen. His reddish brown coat was well groomed and the spikes of fur that ran from the top of his head and down his back were curved and graceful. He sat up on his haunches, his powerful chest and clawed forepaws supporting him in a most majestic and regal way. Around his neck was a velvet cord that carried a large silver pendant, set with an enormous emerald.

"Thank you, Seppish," he said, "That will be all for now."

Seppish nodded and disappeared, leaving Salazar alone with the other waraul.

"Welcome to the Den of the Warauls, young sir," he said, then nodded to one of the pillows opposite him. "Please, sit."

Salazar approached, cautious, and folded his legs to

settle down on the cushion there.

"I am Fildahorr," said the waraul. "Your father has asked me to bring you under my care. He is a good friend to me, as well as my lord, so you will be well taken care of here. I have already had a room prepared for you just down the hall. Before I take you there, there are several things you should know."

The Guardian paused and studied him with shrewd eyes for a moment, then continued,

"You are under no circumstance to attempt to go through the Gate. Is that understood?"

Salazar gave a reluctant nod.

"Good." Fildahorr gave a toothy smile. "It would not be wise for you to go through it now. Perhaps some time later when you have grown older and your father can accompany you. Also, do not go west of here without an escort. That is the territory of the Moranters. They are friends to the Warauls, but they are wary and ever watchful for someone," he paused as if searching for the right word, "*Similar* to you. They would willingly hurt you, perhaps even kill you, without listening to your true identity. Outside of westward, you may go anywhere you wish in the Den or forest; however, be careful. All is not well in the ranks of the Warauls. We have a rogue, Seraphious. He left my group of guardians many years ago, and has taken many with him. We used to number over a thousand, but now... We have not had pups in many centuries. There has been fighting among us and our numbers are but a fraction of what they were. Seraphious is gathering warauls to him, slowly taking my leadership. Be wary, young sir, for he has many of our kind in the woods, and they are silent and may be all too quick to come after you."

Salazar soaked in this information.

"Also," Fildahorr said, "Don't think you will just lounge away your days here, boy." The waraul looked him up and down with a satisfied smile. "Your father has asked that I continue your education. We have also not had a human among us in many years. I'm sure your wonderful asset of hands will prove most useful. Our paws are not as capable as your able limbs. There is work to be done that requires a human's touch. Don't worry, you won't be a slave," the waraul promised with a grin, seeing Salazar's concerned look. "I think you'll find your stay here enjoyable. While we certainly cannot replace your mother and father, I think you will find many a good and loyal friend among us, I being one of them. Come, let me show you around."

The waraul led the boy out into the corridor, motioning down the halls that branched off, saying they were mostly living quarters. The place was enormous, as if a whole castle had been buried under the forest.

Fildahorr led him through the dining hall. There were no tables or chairs, but long pieces of wood, like tabletops, set into the stone floor. Fildahorr only walked on the stone, so Salazar guessed the warauls would sit along the stone and eat off the wood, like flat tables. They went into the kitchen at the back, Fildahorr explaining that warauls preferred their food cooked, but that it took a certain finesse to cook with no hands. Salazar got the feeling he would be asked to help in the kitchen a lot. Fildahorr explained how the smoke was vented up and out into the forest, and how the warauls got most of their food from Etheria; a small party of Etherian soldiers came through once a month with supplies. The Guardian led the boy back out and down the main corridor again, stopping before a door there.

"This will be your room," he said. "Mine is just down the hall, so if you need anything, just come knock."

Fildahorr bowed his head and trotted away, leaving the boy alone. Salazar opened the door and went inside, finding a spacious room. Supporting columns were set into the walls and were carved with twirling vines and lacing knots. Drapes of lush green fabric were hung between them, softening the harsh stone. There was a bucket of water in one corner, and several low bookshelves, though they were mostly empty. There was a long, thick pillow in the back corner with a blanket draped over the end to serve as a bed, and several smaller cushions around the room to sit on. Salazar spied a bag sitting in the middle of the floor, so took a seat on one of the pillows and pulled it over to inspect it.

Salazar's face lit with an excited, relieved smile. Inside the bag were folded most of his clothes, several of his favorite books, and a few small knick-knacks from his room at home. There was also a bow and loaded quiver, a small knife and a short sword. There was a small bag of medicinal herbs and, Salazar was glad to see, a book on how to use them. Having emptied the sack, he tossed it to the side, but paused when it landed with a muffled metallic clink.

Curious, Salazar pulled it back over to him and reached inside, his fingers closing on a large metal circle. He pulled it out to discover it was some kind of pendant. It was perhaps two or three inches in diameter, and though it looked like gold, it was surprisingly light. It was round, hanging from a thick leather cord. At the center was a seven-rayed sun, the crest of his family. Around the edge were strange symbols, and Salazar thought they looked like the ones that had been at the top of the Gate. Tied to the medallion on a thin slip of paper was a line of his father's elegant writing that read: *Ask Fildahorr.*

Salazar held the thing in his hand, thinking he felt a strange prickling sensation on his skin where it touched, and was intrigued. He got to his feet and wandered down the hall to the Guardian's door, where he knocked.

"Come in," came Fildahorr's voice.

Salazar pushed the door open and the waraul looked up with curious eyes.

"This was in my things," the boy said. "My father says to ask you about it." He offered out the pendant for the waraul's inspection.

Fildahorr's eyes widened for a moment, then he gave a slight chuckle.

"It has been millennia since I have seen that," he said. "*That* is the medallion of the Somadar. It belonged to your great-great grandfather, Lu`corian, the second of the seven First. All of the First were capable of wielding great magic, which has been passed down through their bloodlines. Their magic was channeled through a medallion specific to them, which was passed down to their children. Lu`corian's seems to have found its way to your father and now to you."

"You're saying I have magic?" Salazar said, not sure he believed it, "That I can use this to wield it?"

"That is precisely what I'm saying."

"If that's true, why haven't I ever seen magic before? My father has never used any."

"He never had much patience for it," Fildahorr replied with a smile. "Magic is a tedious art. Navar tried to teach your father several times, but he couldn't stand it. Apparently, if he has sent the medallion to you, he thinks you should give it a try."

"Can you teach me?" asked the boy.

"I imagine so. I have no magic myself, but I did know Lu`corian quite well when he was alive."

Salazar couldn't imagine just how *old* the creature before him was.

"But I think that would be best suited for in the morning. You've had a long day, and magic is certainly not something to attempt when one is tired, leastways, not your first attempts anyway."

Chapter Fifteen

That evening, Salazar heard a knock on his door and looked up to see Seppish stick his head inside.

"You will be coming to dinner, won't you?" said the waraul. "We're all heading that way now, if you'd like to join us."

Salazar nodded and rose to go out into the hallway with him. The two made their way toward the dining hall.

"Settling in alright?" Seppish inquired.

"Yes," Salazar replied. "It will take some getting used to, but I think I will like it here."

"No substitute for home, of course," the waraul conceded, "But you won't find one among us who can't sympathize with homesickness."

Salazar gave him a curious look.

"We weren't *always* here, you know," Seppish told him. "Lu`corian appointed our race to guard the Gate. We left Sayden, our beloved home in Etheria, and came here, willing to serve him."

The two entered the dining hall and Seppish trotted over to where Fildahorr was already sitting beside one of the long tabletops set into the floor. Salazar sank down to sit with them.

"Well, there you are," said a reddish colored waraul from Fildahorr's left. "I was beginning to think they were making you up."

"Salazar, this is Azarak," Fildahorr said, casting an irritated eye over at the other waraul. "Azarak, Salazar."

"How do you do?" said Azarak with a broad grin. "So you smote yourself a mortal, eh?"

Fildahorr's head swung over, giving him a horrified look.

"Yes," Salazar admitted, seeing no point in hiding it.

"There are worse things," Azarak said, ignoring Fildahorr. "We get ourselves a mortal from time to time. It happens, I'm afraid, and sometimes it just can't be avoided."

"You will have to join us outside this evening, Salazar," said Fildahorr, changing the subject with a pointed look at Azarak. "We warauls are fine singers and storytellers."

"He does look like Malachi, doesn't he?" mused Azarak, only to be silenced by a nudge and a glare from Fildahorr.

Salazar scowled a bit, not knowing who Malachi might be. Given his chalky white complexion and angular features, Salazar doubted he could resemble anyone very well, except for his own father. Before he could inquire about it, there was a chorus of excited barking as dinner was served.

Chapter Sixteen

Salazar slept little that night, tossing and turning on the pillow, grappling with the blankets. He had stayed up later than he was used to, listening to the warauls sing and spin tales of Etheria and far off places. It was late in the night when he had last flopped on his bed. It was comfortable, but it was not home. He was glad the gold light that illuminated the Den seemed to dim at night, but it was still not as dark as he was accustomed to. He found himself homesick for his own bed, the familiar sounds of the house at night; the wind in the trees outside, the soft footsteps of his father when he rose to stoke the fire in the middle of the night, the chirping of night bugs. It was quiet here. Being underground prevented any sound from outside reaching him. Every now and then, he could hear the muffled clicking of a waraul's claws out in the hall.

He was awake when Seppish nosed the door open in the morning to invite him to breakfast. For all their differences, the warauls seemed to have a very human routine to their lives. The boy even followed Seppish to the same place they had sat for supper the night before. After they had eaten, Fildahorr said to him,

"Come, you and I have things to do."

Salazar followed the waraul out of the dining hall.

"Go and get your medallion," said Fildahorr, "I will come to your room in a moment."

Salazar obeyed, reentering his room and fetching the medallion from the shelf by the bed. Fildahorr came trotting back, a book in his mouth. He set it down on the floor, and nosed it toward the boy.

"Your father wishes me to continue your education," the waraul explained. "I thought perhaps it would be best to capture your interest and then go from there."

Salazar picked up the red leather book, seeing in gold letters, *A History of the Somadàrsath.*

"My family," the boy said, surprised.

"Every member, thoroughly documented and up to date," the waraul replied, seeming proud of the fact. "Your relatives have some interesting stories, which are sure to pique your curiosity about their world, your world. Perhaps then you will not be so averse to studying it."

Salazar cast a suspicious eye over at the Guardian, wondering what his father had told the creature.

"But come, you can read later. This morning, I'd like

to see what you can do with that medallion."

The boy followed him, taking the stairs up out of the Den into the clearing. It was cool and crisp in the morning. The leaves were wet with dew, emanating that earthy smell that Salazar was used to, but the other Immortals seemed to hate. His eyes were drawn to the great arch again and he wandered in closer to it.

"May I ask about that?" he asked, pointing.

"What would you like to know?" Fildahorr replied, sitting back on his haunches.

"What are those symbols? What do they mean?"

"That is the Ancient Etherian language, the language of the First. It used to be the only language in Etheria, until the first mortal went through, then the mortal language caught on, since it was much simpler. Now the Ancient Tongue has been all but forgotten. That line up there reads *Dukéle viatre, en behelendé forvénòn*. Come traveler, and behold eternity."

Salazar's gaze roved over the symbols, feeling something stir in him at the sound of the words Fildahorr spoke. He had never heard them, but there was something familiar in their sound, as if he had known of them before he even had the capacity to know things.

"The circle," said the boy, "What is it?"

"The symbol of Etheria," Fildahorr replied. "The four worlds are each symbolized by a circle."

"Four worlds?" Salazar echoed.

"Indeed." The waraul drew in the dirt with a claw to illustrate. "The white circle is Heaven. The half light and half dark circle is Etheria. The black circle, Earth. The empty circle with the X, Hell."

Fascinated, Salazar extended a hand toward the stone, but Fildahorr barked,

"No! You mustn't touch it!"

"Why?"

"It will open the Gate."

For a moment, Salazar had the urge to thrust his hand forward, but he thought better of it and withdrew.

"Do you go through often?" asked the boy.

"No," Fildahorr replied. "It is rare that I leave Earth anymore. I used to go through every few months to make reports, but now I send someone else in my stead. The last time I went personally was when I had to tell your father that Galator had come through."

The waraul stood and trotted away down the clearing. Salazar was reluctant to follow, wanting more than anything to lunge at the Gate. Nonetheless, he followed the Guardian to where the two sat down in a secluded corner of the clearing.

"The first thing you must know about magic," Fildahorr began. "Is that it has no morals, no virtues, no sense of right or wrong. Magic can be used for good or for evil depending on its wielder. It can become good or evil, orderly or chaotic, when it is bound to a wielder, but in its raw form it has no alignment whatsoever. It can be an immensely powerful art and you must never let that power go to your head. You are blessed, Salazar, for few humans can do any kind of magic. Only those descended of the First and a handful of lucky people are capable of it. The only race with any consistent kind of magic is the Unicorns, who can heal wounds and purify water, but that is generally the extent of their power. The Dragons have a bit of magic as well, though it varies more between the individuals. But you, young one, can wield this ancient and sacred power to the fullest extent. You must always remember, however, just because you *can* do something, does not necessarily mean that you *should*. You have been given a great gift. All of the power of your forefathers lies within you. All you must do is connect to it."

"How do I do that?" Salazar asked.

"It would be far easier to do in Etheria, but I imagine you can still manage it here. Close your eyes," Fildahorr instructed. "Hold the medallion in your hand."

Salazar did so, feeling ridiculous. He hoped none of the other warauls could see him. His fingers wrapped around the cool metal of the medallion and he awaited Fildahorr's next instruction.

"Quiet your mind," Fildahorr said. "There is a deepness within your soul, a cool, calming, well of power. Can you feel it?"

"No," Salazar muttered, still feeling ridiculous and awkward.

"If you're worried about the others seeing you," Fildahorr said, as if reading his thoughts, "They won't care. You humans are such self-conscious creatures. Calm yourself. Listen to the wind in the trees, feel the world beneath you, feel the Gate just there and the power that comes from it. Search deep inside yourself and find the deepness that is there."

Salazar did as the Guardian instructed. He realized he had begun to breathe deeper, more slowly. He heard the wind rustling in the leaves around him and could hear one of the warauls laughing a short distance away. The coolness of the morning air crept in around him and it was as though he could *feel* the Gate there on the other side of the clearing. It was as if it were the center of ripples spreading out over water, calling him to it. That same feeling crept up in him, but stronger, like some lost corner of his soul was awakening, something older than he could imagine, something that made him feel small and powerful all at once.

"Do you feel it?"

"Yes," Salazar whispered, as if afraid a sound might

scare the feeling away.

"Now, keep your eyes closed," Fildahorr nosed through the leaves and clamped a small pebble in his teeth and tossed it out in front of Salazar, "Call the pebble into your hand. Become one with the power within you, feel it flow through you, feel it pool around the medallion, use the metal to direct it. Reach out and feel the pebble with your mind. Examine it, its curves, its shape, and call it."

Salazar thought it was ridiculous to think he would be able to see something with his eyes closed, but as he sat there, he *did*. It was not so much *seeing* and it was he simply became aware of the pebble there in front of him. He could sense its pale smooth sides, how it had been crushed at one end. It was a wild sensation; everything in him said it should not be possible, and yet, there was the image of the pebble in his mind, as clear as if he had seen Fildahorr toss it down. *Come,* he thought to it, *Come here.*

Nothing happened, but Salazar was unperturbed. He focused in on the image in his mind, clamping his thoughts around it and commanded, *Come to me.*

There! A wobble. The stone shifted in the leaves as if nudged by an invisible finger. Determined not to let it go, Salazar pulled against the power at the back of his mind, dragging it out to where he could access it, feeling it pulse through his veins. He could feel the medallion in his hand, imagining that his skin tingled around it. Grabbing onto the pebble with his thoughts, he demanded, *Come!*

The pebble shifted there on the ground, then lifted, very slowly, as if carried by an unseen hand. There was a clink as it dropped onto the medallion in his palm and Salazar's eyes snapped open, stunned.

"I got it," he breathed. He looked up to Fildahorr, amazed. "I got it!"

"So you did," said the waraul with a proud smile. "Very good indeed. Now that you have felt what it is like to summon magic, you should practice. *Only* practice moving things for now. I'll tell you how to handle other things later."

With that, the waraul rose and trotted away, leaving the boy alone with the magic.

Chapter Seventeen

Seraphious awoke to hear a pair of voices hissing,

"Don't wake him—"

"He'll want to know—"

"It can wait—"

"Are you sure—"

"*What?*" Seraphious demanded.

The two warauls fell silent as their large golden brown leader emerged from his den. He stood over them by at least a full head and looked down at them through narrowed yellow eyes.

"There is news from the Tress," said one of the warauls before him. "I thought you'd want to know as soon as—"

"What is it?" Seraphious growled.

"There is a human with them. Salazar Somadàrsath, heir of Lask."

Seraphious cocked his head, surprised.

"He will be with them for several years as I understand," the waraul continued, "Exiled from Letiana, though his father is still obligated to stay there."

"What should we do?" asked the other. "He could be dangerous. If—"

"Do nothing," Seraphious replied. "Keep out of his sight as you do the guardians'. No one is to go near him and I will personally skin anyone who tries to hurt him. We can't afford to have his father get involved here or find out. It is shame and desire for vengeance that keeps Fildahorr quiet. We cannot let a boy endanger that."

Chapter Eighteen

Salazar loved magic. He couldn't understand why his father would not want anything to do with it. The boy spent hours outside and inside, working with the magic every day until he could pick up things with his mind without even needing to close his eyes. It was great fun. Within several weeks, he had even rearranged the furniture in his room. Once he got used to the sensation, it became easy. He could even manage moving two smaller things at the same time. Fildahorr was very impressed.

After those weeks, the boy realized he was exhausted. It was all he could do to get out of bed in the mornings and keep himself sitting upright at dinner. Fildahorr chuckled and explained that too much magic could have a very real tax on the body, especially at first, and recommended he spend at least a day or two doing no magic at all.

"You might have told me sooner," the boy muttered.

He did not join the warauls outside that evening, going instead to collapse out on his bed in an exhausted daze.

Several days later, once he was rested, Fildahorr taught the boy how to manipulate light, conjure it from nothing, or harness and shape it from sources around oneself. By the end of the day, the boy was fashioning many illusions out of the golden light of the Den, fascinating the warauls who stuck their heads into his room to watch.

Chapter Nineteen

"Are you nervous?" asked Fildahorr.

"Not particularly," Seraphious replied as they trotted toward the Gate. "Are you?"

"We're leaving Etheria, most likely for good," said Fildahorr. "We'll never live in Sayden again. Guarding the Gate is a huge responsibility." He paused. "He's choosing today, you know."

"Yes, but I'm not nervous about that either."

"I look for it to be you," Fildahorr said with a smile. "You're much stronger and faster than most of us. You're well liked—"

"So are you." Seraphious said it, if only to make his friend feel better. Seraphious believed himself to be the better candidate, both by strength and leadership, and was confident Lu`corian would think the same.

"Let's make a promise," Fildahorr said. "No matter what happens, we'll still be best friends."

"I should think that would go unspoken," Seraphious

replied with a grin. "And if I *am* chosen, you will be my second in command."

"Likewise," Fildahorr agreed.

They followed behind the last of the warauls there, entering the shining golden light, crossing through to Earth. The clearing was a flurry of activity as the warauls were entering the newly-built Den, taking up stations around the perimeter, helping to move supplies. A small number had congregated around one of the few humans there.

He was a tall, proud man, with frosty white skin and hair, dressed in silver and blue. He looked up as the last of the warauls arrived and motioned Fildahorr and Seraphious over. They came and sat back on their haunches before him, subjecting themselves to his scarlet-eyed inspection.

"It is good to see both of you," said Lu`corian. "I suppose there is no time to waste." He reached into his pocket and withdrew a large silver pendant set with a shining emerald. "I reviewed each of you carefully and it was not an easy choice to make. You are both fine warauls. The responsibility of being the Guardian will be no easy task and it will demand very much of you."

Seraphious sat a little straighter, pricking his ears, anticipating and wanting to look ready. Fildahorr glanced at him.

"So," Lu`corian was continuing, "I wish you the best of luck, Fildahorr." He smiled and knelt, placing the pendant around Fildahorr's neck.

"I shall defend the Gate til my dying breath, Somadar," Fildahorr promised.

"And Etheria shall thank you for it."

Lu`corian rose and told Seraphious,

"And you shall make a fine advisor to him. The Gate will be doubly safe under both of your watchful gazes."

Seraphious bowed his head, but cast a sidelong look at Fildahorr, who sat with his head up and chest out, looking satisfied.

Chapter Twenty

Magic was the perfect diversion. Salazar felt like he always had something to do, so he found himself free of homesickness altogether. The Den was a fascinating new place, and every day, he and Fildahorr would take a walk through the forest. The boy would listen to the waraul speak of Etheria and its history and Salazar found the stories fascinating. They were the same as the ones Lask had told him, but being so near the Gate and among another race suddenly made them much more real.

In the afternoons, Salazar would curl up in his room with the book Fildahorr had given him and read about his family. It made the history lessons Fildahorr insisted on giving him more bearable. The boy endured the warauls' teachings, if only to get to the magic lessons faster. The weeks progressed quickly and soon Fildahorr chanced teaching the boy about fire magic. Outside of one unfortunate drapery in his room, Salazar got the hang of it with minimal trouble and Fildahorr was very proud of him.

Each day was a new adventure for the boy and it wasn't long until he had fallen into the step of life among the Warauls. At night, in the quiet, darkened hours when the Den was still, the boy would feel the absence of his parents and long for his familiar bed, but when morning came, the warauls saw to it that he was kept much too busy to be homesick.

Chapter Twenty-One

Myranda awoke and knew that it was still very early, perhaps an hour yet before dawn. She had slept only a little, as she had the past few weeks. She could hear the quiet, rhythmic breath of Lask who slept beside her and felt its warmth fan across her collarbone from where his head rested against her shoulder. Her fingers brushed over his head, smoothing down his soft hair where it had been tousled as he slept.

Myranda knew she would not sleep any more, and so shifted free of Lask, slowly, so not to wake him, and slipped out of bed. The floor was cold under her feet, but she did not notice it, going over to light one of the candles from the still glowing embers in the small fireplace on the other side of the room. She sat down in the chair there, setting the candle on the low table, and rubbed a hand over her face.

It was like there was a hole in the back of her mind, a

dark emptiness where once the warm light of Salazar had been. Myranda's fingers found their way to the necklace she had taken off and set on the table the day before. It was a pretty thing; gold, open-worked, with fine leaves. It was set with six small rubies, and at the center, an enormous pearl. Lask had given it to her on their wedding day, saying it was the very pearl that had caused his forefather Lu`corian to be cursed and all of his sons to be pale and red-eyed. Lu`corian had given it to his wife, Mara, and ever since, it had been passed down through the family, always adorning the wife of the Somadar. There were tiny symbols around the edge of the pendant; Aetherian letters, Lask had told her. When she asked what they said, he had replied, *Somadaré Amanthiel*, the heart of the Somadar.

Myranda gave a faint smile, tracing a finger over the smooth pearl. She glanced back toward the bed, where Lask slept. His arm had stretched out over the other side of the bed, seeking her even in his sleep. There had been a time when Myranda thought she would never be unhappy again, that she would never feel lonely or frightened so long as Lask was there. He was a good husband and a fine companion, but in the past few weeks, she had borne a sadness that even he could not comfort.

She glanced back down to the pendant. Lask had given her many things since she had married him, even Immortality itself, but she found herself thinking that the greatest thing they had ever given each other was Salazar.

Myranda got to her feet and slipped out of the room without a sound, going across the hall and entering her son's room. It was empty, devoid not only of the boy, but many of his belongings as well. For a moment, she stood there, looking around as if lost, then went over to the bed and curled up on it, resting her head on the pillow, trying to take a bit of comfort in lying where her only child had lain.

She curled herself up tighter, the tears slipping silently down her face as she ran a hand over the mattress beside her, wanting so much to find the familiar back under her fingers that she had so often stroked while he slept. She did not know how long she lay there, closing her eyes and just running her fingers over the empty place beside her. In time, she heard a quiet voice say,

"Myranda?"

She opened her eyes to see Lask there in the doorway.

"Darling, what are you doing?" he asked, though she could tell by the pain in his voice he already knew.

Myranda knew she must look pathetic, but she couldn't stop the tears. She shut her eyes again, hardly able to look at him, seeing Salazar in his pale face.

Lask came and sank down onto the bed, laying himself out beside her so he could pull her into his embrace.

"We'll see him again soon," Lask told her. He pulled her face up to look at him and wiped the tears from her face. "Please don't cry, love," he murmured, "I can't bear to see you cry." He kissed her forehead. "It won't be long til the Senate meeting, then we'll go see him—"

"Almost two months," Myranda sniffed.

Lask stroked her face with his thumb, not knowing what to say to comfort her. He glanced up to the pale, faint light of dawn beginning to filter through the trees outside.

"What would you like for breakfast?" he asked, kissing her cheek. "I'll make it."

"I'll do it," Myranda said, shaking her head.

Lask tried to keep her there against him, but Myranda struggled free of him, standing up and rubbing a hand over her face to scrub away the tearstains. She stormed out of the room and Lask lay there, looking up at the ceiling, at a loss. He felt the absence of Salazar as much as she did, but perhaps it was his eight hundred and nine years of life that made two months not seem as long.

After a moment, he got to his feet and went to the kitchen, expecting to see Myranda hacking at the fruit or shredding the bread, but instead, he found her crumpled to the floor, sitting with her back against the counter, face buried in her hands while the tears streamed through her fingers.

The sight put a knife in Lask's heart and he swept over, sinking to his knees before her. He tugged gently at her wrists, trying to pull her hands away from her face, but Myranda shook her head, pulling back from him.

"Darling, please," Lask whispered and pulled her to him. She hid herself against him and Lask could feel her trembling there in his arms. "What can I do?" he asked, voice quiet. "Tell me. I'll do it."

Myranda just huddled there against him. Lask kissed her head.

"I will tell Tephanis I have been summoned back to Etheria for an urgent meeting with the king," he said. "We can leave this afternoon, make our way north, stay at the Gate for a few days—"

"You'd lie to the king?"

"He is not my king."

Chapter Twenty-Two

Salazar was sitting among the warauls by the fire. They seemed particularly nostalgic, speaking of their home in Sayden, singing sad songs of longing. It wasn't long until the usual argument ensued over what story Arra should tell.

"Tell us about how the warauls found Sayden," said Avamor.

"No, no, about the day Fah Ling arrived in Etheria!"

"We just heard that one! How about the demon of Castar's Pool?"

"The haunted mountain of Ilvastris!"

"Tell the creation story," said Salazar. All the warauls looked at him. "I'd like to hear about the creation of Etheria." He had heard the story from his father, but was curious to hear how the warauls would present it.

"Well have at it, Arra," barked Azarak.

Hearing no more resistance, Arra smiled and began,

"In the beginning, long before the worlds were put in motion, there was nothing, only the Great One and the Void. The Creator grew weary of the nothingness and so commanded there to be light, and so there was light; there were stars. From the dust of the stars, He formed the worlds, countless, endless places traveling in the Void. One of them, however, split itself in two, remaining joined by magic, yet they formed separate worlds. The Creator took pity on the smaller world, but a tiny corner of the greater whole, and He blessed it, fashioning it after Heaven itself and summoning the Spring of Life to flow there. The land would be forever young, its children immune to the toll of Time.

Into this land he placed the seven Ancients and the seven First, each of whom was given a specific task. The Ancients had their functions and the First their duties. Together, they would shape the world into what we know today, living for one hundred years in direct contact with the Creator, learning all about the world, setting up the society that still exists today, preparing the world for the rest of the races that would live there. Though the imperfect nature of all creatures has caused war and strife, the world remains relatively unchanged; the descendents of the First still reign and Etheria remains a paradise as it was created to be."

The warauls all had a distant look in their eyes. Blair

heaved a wistful sigh. One of them started singing,

"Hearken now, o'er the mountains calling,
Voices sing in an ageless light.
Theirs is the song of wind and water,
The spark that blazes within each soul.
Hear their song and keep it true,
Hold it close inside your heart,
Ne'er forget those who've gone before you
In the land of Etheria!

Listen now, hear the waters crashing,
On the white shores of the sea.
See the sun rising in the East sky,
Moonset falling upon the West,
While the stars shine down in glory,
Blazing out in darkest night.
Light shall e'er triumph over darkness
In the land of Etheria!

Feel the wind soaring out to meet you,
Hear the trees sigh as it passes by,
Their bright leaves shining in the morning,
Glist'ning in the earliest dew.
And so hear the birds a-calling,
Singing out a merry song.

Hear them sing, 'We shall always love thee,
Blessed land of Etheria!'

Call we now, 'all creatures unite,
Stand ye strong against all your foes.'
All sad divisions may we cease
To defend our beloved land.
May we ever stand together,
Sharing in each other's strength.
Hear our cry, 'Not even death can break us
In our land of Etheria!'"

Salazar sat in silence, listening to the harmonized voices of the warauls in the tune that rang with a haunting beauty, something strangely familiar, yet otherworldly. He had read the words long ago in one of his father's books, though his father said they didn't carry the same rhythm and rhyme as they did in the Aetherian tongue. He had heard his father hum the tune once in a while as he worked, but never had the boy heard the two together. Something in the melody brought an ache to his chest, a cold, desperate homesickness, not for Letiana or the home with his parents, but for a land he had never even seen.

It was the strangest sensation, being unable to imagine something, yet wanting it more than he had ever wanted anything. It was as if his very blood ached with the absence of Etheria around him, a pain that seemed to well up in the very bottom of his soul.

Even after he curled up in his bed and lay there trying to sleep, he could still feel that terrible longing. The fact the Gate was so close just made it all the worse. All it would take was a touch of his hand and he could quench the desperate thirst in his soul. Surely he could find a way to sneak past the guards at the Gate. Or suppose he didn't sneak at all?

An idea slithered into his mind, and a faint, crooked smile found its way onto his face as the boy worked over the notion. He waited until he was sure it was very late, unable to sleep because of the nervous energy twitching through him. When he knew several hours had passed, Salazar rose, not bothering with his shoes, and went out into the darkness.

He sauntered over toward the Gate and sank down between the two guards there.

"What's the matter?" asked Seppish. "Can't sleep?"

"No. Why are you guarding so late?" asked Salazar, surprised to see the waraul out at this hour.

"Lost a game of bones," the waraul muttered.

"Well *I* wouldn't have a problem sleeping," said the other waraul, face pulling back into a wide yawn.

"Why don't you go sleep then?" Salazar suggested.

"I'm awake anyway. I could take your shift."

The waraul looked around him, with suddenly eager eyes, toward Seppish.

"Go on then," said Seppish, shaking his head.

"Thanks," the waraul said, giving the boy a grateful nudge. He trudged away toward the Den.

"Very kind of you," Seppish remarked.

"If I'm awake anyway, I might as well make myself useful," the boy said. He glanced over at the waraul. "What do you do out here all night?"

"Stargaze, swap stories, tell jokes that only make sense when you're dreadfully tired."

Salazar looked skyward, and though he already knew, he asked,

"What are those constellations there?"

Seppish looked up, taking stock of the sky.

"That cross there is Cygnus, one of my favorites..."

The waraul was continuing, but Salazar wasn't paying attention. He felt around in the leaves behind him until his fingers closed around a thick rock. Making sure the waraul was still preoccupied with the stars, he tossed it away into the leaves to the side, making Seppish start and swing his head over toward the sound.

"What was that?" hissed the waraul.

"I don't know," Salazar replied.

"You stay here. I'll go check with the perimeter."

Salazar watched him trot away into the shadows, following the brush wall around until he disappeared from sight. Not wasting a moment, Salazar scrambled to his feet and hesitated for only a second before he thrust his hand out to rest upon the cold green stone.

A blinding gold light flared under the arch, filling the opening. It flowed around upon itself like water and it rippled under the single finger that Salazar touched to it. Knowing the waraul would be sprinting in his direction, he could not waste much time looking at it. Throwing caution to the winds, he flung himself forward into the shining portal.

There was nothing. No sound, no color, no feeling, only the flat grey Void. Salazar looked around in the emptiness and down at himself to see that his skin had taken on the grey hue of his surroundings. He got the distinct feeling of rising, as if he were weightless, floating up like smoke, though he felt no wind from the motion on his skin, nor observed anything passing him. The utter silence was terrifying. His senses were scrambling for something to grasp. He could not even hear his own heartbeat, though he felt it spasming in his chest. What if he had done something wrong? What if he was trapped in the greyness, a prisoner of nothing? What if—

Without warning, the grey seemed to lurch and all of a sudden he stumbled forward to stand on solid ground once more and all the sounds and smells came rushing back to him.

It was like some foggy curtain had been pulled back. The night was soft and velveteen. Even in the darkness, the colors were vibrant; lush greens and blues and violets. The silver shimmer of moonlight cast everything in a delicate glow. The grass beneath his feet was soft as silk, the short, emerald green stalks brushing against his toes like feathers.

He found himself standing before a green stone arch, twin to the one on Earth, though he now stood among trees prouder than any he could have imagined. They were impossibly tall and broad, ancient beyond his measure, straight and graceful, with leaves trimmed in gold that whispered in the warm breeze. On the wind was such a scent, some heavenly perfume that not even the most beautiful of women would be worthy to wear. There was a sweet floral fragrance, coupled with a fresh, crisp spice that filled the lungs like a breath of cold autumn air.

Salazar turned his eyes skyward and gasped, his awe complete as he beheld the heavens. The richest, darkest violet stretched like velvet above the treetops, sprayed with such an endless number of brilliant stars the boy could only stand beneath them, feeling tiny.

The world felt rich and ancient, yet young and spry all at once. As he stood there, Salazar felt a joy well up in his soul, and he decided that he had never known what *home* truly felt like until this moment. It was as if everything had suddenly snapped into crystal clarity. Everything that had ever been wrong no longer mattered. Nothing he had ever done or ever wanted to do, could compare to the absolute fulfilling peace that swept over him as he stood among those trees.

A heavy weight plowed into him from behind, shoving him down into the grass, and Salazar felt claws digging into his shoulders and hot breath on his neck.

"Fool of a boy!" snarled Fildahorr's voice. "What were you *thinking*? Get up!"

The Guardian stepped back, allowing the boy to haul himself to his feet.

"What the devil do you think you're doing?" the waraul growled, tall ears flattened back against his head.

"I just wanted to see it—"

"Well you've seen it. Take a good look, boy, it's the last you'll be getting for a long while."

"Why are you so determined to keep me from this place?" Salazar demanded.

"Because it's not *safe*!" Fildahorr barked. "When you are older and wiser you will venture here. All is not well in this land! There are those who would gladly take you, *kill* you even, to gain leverage over your father! You're lucky I managed to follow you so quickly, and lucky that you didn't wander from the Gate."

Salazar glanced up to the archway, noticing the circle at its peak was all black and the symbols beneath it were different.

"Now come," growled Fildahorr, turning around to touch a paw to the stone, making the arch fill with light once more, "We're going home."

"No," said Salazar, planting his feet, "I'm here. I'm going to have a look around."

"You will come back to Earth *this instant*, boy, or so help me—"

"What?" snapped Salazar. "What can you do? I have more right than you to be here and you have been telling me all this time that I am of a noble line, practically a prince in my own way. This is *my* home and I will return with you, but not until I'm good and ready."

"Insolent boy! Your father—"

"Is not here," Salazar finished. "And I am *going* to have a look at this place *tonight*, so you can either come with me or I will go on my own."

With that, that boy turned and marched off into the trees.

"*Get back here*!" Fildahorr roared.

Salazar took off at a run, hearing the Guardian's irate howl of,

"SALAZAR!"

The boy did not slow down. He was tired of being kept in the dark and sick of everyone keeping him from the one place he was meant to be. As he wove through the trees, he looked over his shoulder to see if Fildahorr was pursuing him, but saw no sign of the waraul.

There was a strange sound then; a deep, rhythmic thumping, like the beat of an enormous unseen heart.

There was a rush of wind and a giant golden shape plummeted out of the sky. Salazar was knocked off his feet, finding himself pinned beneath an enormous scaly foot, two black claws piercing into the ground on either side of his head. He looked up, stunned and terrified, into the face of a dragon.

It held its head with a sort of skeptical pride, its golden scales less lustrous in the darkness. Two black horns grew back from the top of its head and a proud, leathery crest fanned from the top of its head down its neck. Its coppery wings flared and blocked out the stars, while its spiked tail swung back and forth behind it, like an irritated cat's. It narrowed bright green eyes at him.

"Well, well," it said, and Salazar was surprised at how smooth and obviously female its voice was, "What have we here? A pasty little two-legger running full tilt from the Gate? Dear me, those green eyes could only belong to one— though you look younger, Malachi, how ever did you manage that?"

"Who?" squeaked Salazar, thinking this creature could probably swallow him whole.

The dragon did not look amused.

"We all know you're not stupid, Malachi," she said, "So don't even bother playing that game."

"Who is Malachi?" the boy demanded. "I'm Salazar!"

The dragon snorted in surprise, a puff of smoke billowing from her nostrils and making the boy cough.

"NO, SCOARIN!" came a shout. "Don't hurt him!"

Fildahorr came bounding up to the pair, saying,

"Don't hurt him. He is Lask's son."

"So I've just learned," rumbled the dragon.

"*So let him up,*" the waraul hissed, fur bristling.

"If you insist," said Scoarin with a pointy-toothed grin, and raised her foot.

Salazar scrambled out from under it and got to his feet, looking up at her in both awe and fear.

"Never seen a dragon, I suppose," she remarked at his stare. She glanced over to Fildahorr. "And just what are the two of you doing here so late?"

"The boy snuck through the Gate," growled Fildahorr. "And then had the audacity to run from me."

"Only because *you* and everyone else had the *audacity* to tell me I belong here yet never let me see it," the boy shot back and returned the waraul's glare.

"I see," hummed Scoarin. "Well, Fildahorr, I must say

the boy seems to have a fair argument."

"You *cannot* think it wise for him to be wandering around by himself in the middle of the night when Vortearigan's spies could be anywhere."

"Oh honestly, Fildahorr, I think Vortearigan's agents have better things to do than wander the Carthonian in hopes of snagging a boy who's not even supposed to be here. Beside, he's not alone." She extended a hand to the boy. "Hop on then, Salazar, I'll show you around."

Salazar approached her hand, deciding he liked this dragon very much.

"Scoarin!" Fildahorr barked. "He has disobeyed both me and the wishes of his father and *you're* taking him for a little stroll!"

"Little flight, actually. There's no point in coming all this way and then just leaving. You're in charge of guarding the Gate and the boy slipped past all your defenses. I think he's beaten you fair enough, and the victor ought to claim his prize."

Fildahorr snarled, teeth bared and ears flat in an expression of utter fury.

"Oh don't lose your fur," said the dragon, scooping the boy up and setting him on her shoulders between the spikes that ran along her spine. "I'll have him back on Earth before sunup."

Fildahorr glared up at Salazar, growling,

"You and I are going to have a very long talk when you return."

Salazar did not reply, nor did Scoarin give him a chance to. With a push from her back legs and a pump of her wings, she launched them into the air, flapping above the treetops.

It was amazing. Salazar could see for miles in the clear night air. The moonlight illuminated the shimmering forest below, the elegant branches reaching up as if to caress the stars.

"The Carthonian Forest," said Scoarin, "Owned and overseen by your father. It is also where he, and all of your forefathers, grew up." The dragon glanced back at him.

The boy realized he had heard of Scoarin many times in his father's stories, but had always sort of dismissed her as a fictional character. It was all real; he was flying on the back of the proof. He could feel Scoarin's great body moving beneath him, muscles working, scales shifting in fluid rhythmic strokes. Salazar looked down to see they were following the path of a shining river that wound through the trees below them.

"Hold on," said Scoarin.

Without any further warning, she tucked her wings tight against her sides and plunged straight down the great height of an enormous waterfall. Salazar let out a yelp of surprise but his panic was replaced by the glorious feeling of falling. He had to lean back against her spike and clutch the one behind it to keep from falling off. The cold mist sprayed his skin in a crystalline delight bringing up goosebumps from the rushing air as they passed through a faint moonlit rainbow. Suddenly, Scoarin flared her wings and pulled up just above the river, claws splashing in the crystal water, and soared back up into the sky, flapping eastward. Salazar leaned forward, flinging his arms out as if to embrace the whole world and threw back his head to let out a triumphant howl of delight. He felt Scoarin's sides shake under his legs as a chuckle rolled through her.

"That was the Falls of Eshalloth," she told him, "The largest waterfall in Etheria. The caves behind it were once home to the dragon Navar, and where your father was raised." She looked back at him, smiling at the look of wonder on the boy's face as his eyes roamed everywhere around them. "What would you like to see?" she asked. "The High Peaks where the Griffins dwell or the Finistriel Forest of the Fairies? Or perhaps the Plain of Camulis where the Centaurs roam or to the villages around the castle like Delures or Denmahi?"

"Oh I don't care," Salazar breathed, "Just so long as I'm here."

Scoarin chuckled again and banked east, tail swinging behind her like a rudder. Salazar watched the ancient trees swish by beneath them until they thinned out into a field and he saw a castle there. Its pale walls were almost white in the moonlight, with tall turrets roofed with blue slate tiles. It was an enormous, grand place, and he could see the long pennants drifting in the breeze at the top of each tower and the banners flapping from the walls.

"The castle of the High King," said Scoarin, "Home of King Lavancer, the only man in all the kingdom your father must answer to, though you'd hardly know it, as they are the best of friends. One day you will go there and your father will formally present you as his heir before the Senate."

Salazar could hardly wrap his mind around it. The thought of belonging here, of helping to rule it, was such a thrilling (and intimidating) prospect. Scoarin banked again, soaring to the south. Salazar saw a glimmer in the distance, and as they came closer, he realized it was a city; a great, beautiful place, with proud towers, and clean streets that wound among long blocks of shops and houses. What struck the boy most was how decorated it was. No building was without sculpture or wood carvings or bright painted designs. The Etherians had such an obvious love of beauty, even their common architecture looked like a work of art.

"Denmahi, favored city of your father," Scoarin told

him. "One of the largest cities in Etheria, second only to Arajei, the port city far to the south. It would take us at least a day to fly there, else I would surely show it to you."

The dragon caught a warm updraft, soaring on past the city, whisking them away to the southeast. Salazar leaned back against the spike behind him, breathing deep of the crisp air, wondering if a person could die of contentment. He did not know how long they flew, but Salazar was too enthralled to care. This place surpassed all of Arra's descriptions and every story his father had ever told him. At length Scoarin's flight slowed and she said,

"Look down."

Salazar pulled his gaze away from the stars and looked down into a large clearing below them, where there slept a herd of horses. No, not horses—

"Unicorns," said the dragon.

They slept curled in unsurpassed grace, each spiral horn glistening in the moonlight. They were an array of colors: white, chestnut, black, gold, silver, some even having tints of purple and blue, each just as beautiful and stunning as its fellows. They radiated serenity in their sleep and Salazar saw one look up at Scoarin before lying back down to rest.

Scoarin turned and flew south for a while longer until Salazar saw a fire in the distance. When they came closer he could see shapes sleeping around the campfire and several guards on horseback watching the perimeter. Only the guards weren't *on* horseback, Salazar realized as they drew closer, they were *attached* to horse bodies.

"Centaurs," Scoarin said.

Salazar marveled at the beings below him, wondering how such strange creatures could be real. They looked up at the dragon, and Salazar could see tall pointy ears prick up through their thick manes of hair.

"Dawn approaches," Scoarin said, pulling Salazar out of his wondering, "You must return to Earth."

She turned her flight to the northwest and quickened her pace, finding a wind to help propel her along. Salazar was reminded of the reality he would soon have to face. He thought of Fildahorr waiting, seething, when he returned and wondered what the Guardian would do to him.

"Do I have to go back?" he asked the dragon, "Could I just stay with you?"

"I'm afraid Fildahorr would never consent to that," Scoarin said with a chuckle, "It is best if you return to the mortal realms for a time."

"But Fildahorr—"

"Oh you'll get a right good lecture when you get back, but just sit and nod and say it won't happen again and all will be well in a few days," she said. "Fildahorr's a soft one at heart. He can't stay angry long, especially with people he likes. He'll be furious, of course, when you get back, but it will be over soon enough. Besides, you got to see Etheria, isn't that worth his ire?"

"Of course," Salazar agreed, without hesitating, "But I won't come back until Adar is with me now that I've seen it. I just wanted to know it truly existed and what it was like. No one wanted me to know, so I went by myself."

"I can't blame you," Scoarin said. "I probably would have too. You're so much like your father when he was your age. How he and Forge could frustrate Navar." She paused, seeming to be lost in a memory, then murmured, "No doubt Lask pines for this land even more than you do. How long do you think it will be before he returns? Twenty, fifty years?"

"I hope not that long!" Salazar exclaimed. "I'll be an old man by then!"

"Oh Salazar," Scoarin chuckled, "You have an eternity before you. Fifty years is little more than a week or so after you've lived as long as I."

"How long *have* you lived?"

"I am about three thousand years old."

"Three *thousand*?"

"Yes, and Fildahorr is even older."

Salazar gaped.

"See? Fifty years is not so long to wait."

Chapter Twenty-Three

Salazar sat in awkward silence before Fildahorr's scrutinizing glare. The Guardian's dark eyes blazed and were boring a hole into the boy, though Salazar managed to hold his gaze.

"Do you fully understand what you did tonight?" Fildahorr asked. Without giving the boy time to reply, he continued, "Let me explain it to you. First off, you deceived my guards, and that in itself was a very disgraceful thing to do, particularly for one of your lineage. Second, you broke one of the few rules I asked you to abide by during your stay here. I do not ask for much, Salazar, in return for watching over you and providing for you, but the one thing I did ask was that you *not go through the Gate*!" His voice rose to a sharp bark at these last words. "Nevertheless, you did. As if that was not bad enough, you proceeded to openly defy me, turn your back and run from me. You ran into Scoarin, where you undermined my authority and took off on your little jaunt—"

"That was *her* idea," Salazar interrupted in his defense.

"But you did not have to take her offer!" Fildahorr retorted. "Whether you like it or not, Salazar, you are under my control. You may be of a noble bloodline, but you are not a lord yet. Your father, however, is and I must answer to him for your safety. He charged me with your welfare, which means, boy, you *listen to me.* I may not be your father, but you still have to treat my word as though I were. We do not have to be enemies, if anything I hope to be one of your best friends, but even in friendship you must still remember that I am, for now, your superior and my word is as good as law to you; particularly when it is something with as much importance as the Gate and Etheria. My duty is to protect the Gate, even if it means I must protect it from you—"

"I told you when I first arrived here that if you would let me get one glimpse of my world I would never try to go through the Gate or pester you about it. You denied that to me and I eventually had to take it into my own hands." He paused and mustered the courage to say, "Even if that meant disobeying you."

"Young and foolish human," Fildahorr growled, "You are arrogant and naïve. If you had waited til you were older—"

"Why?" Salazar demanded. "Because of a few enemies that might be roaming around? Because of Vortregar—"

"Vortearigan—"

"Whoever! I don't care who or what might be out there, but that is *my* world and no man or beast on this Earth is going to keep me from it!"

"Boldly spoken for one of only thirteen years," Fildahorr hissed.

"Just because I'm young to you doesn't mean that gives you the right to treat me any less than one of your own! Maybe in Etheria I would be a baby, but here in this world I am older and capable of understanding things if you would only tell me!"

"Do you speak to your father like this?" Fildahorr asked.

"*Yes,*" Salazar retorted. "And we have a similar argument quite often."

"Lask must have the patience of a saint," Fildahorr muttered under his breath. The waraul closed his eyes and heaved a heavy sigh. "What's done is done," he said, "And there's no changing what happened. You've had your glimpse, and I expect that you will do no such thing ever again."

"I won't," Salazar promised.

"You'd best not, boy," the Guardian warned, "And we will need to work on your respect of me."

"I'm sorry," Salazar sighed, "I didn't particularly *like* having to disregard you and I'm sorry that I did and I won't do it again, but… I had to."

Fildahorr gazed at him for a long time, observing, scrutinizing, calculating. Such a gaze made Salazar uneasy, though he held the waraul's dark stare and tried to show no sign of his anxiety.

"I forgive you," Fildahorr said at length, "I suppose. Though I do not approve of your actions, I cannot deny I may have done the same for the love of my world. Etheria is perfect. It is what most on this Earth only dream of. I do not see it as often as I'd like and if everyone around me had and they always spoke of how wonderful it was and I was always told I belonged there yet no one would let me see it… I might have done the same. I cannot be but so angry with you knowing that my course of action would have been similar."

For a moment, Salazar was stunned.

"This surprises you, I see," the Guardian said. "It is your first offense, albeit a severe one. You have done nothing else wrong while you've been here, I can relate as to why you did, and I happen to like you. So, you are forgiven. Just *don't* do it again and from now on you *listen* to me when I tell you things."

Chapter Twenty-Four

Seraphious paused outside the door trying to think of what he wanted to say. Not wanting to be caught lingering there, he took a breath and scratched at the door with a paw.

"Come in," came Fildahorr's voice. He looked up and smiled when Seraphious came inside. "Ah, good morning!"

Seraphious gave an amiable smile, settling down on the pillow across from him.

"Something on your mind?" Fildahorr asked, reading his expression instantly.

"Yvana came to speak to you the day before yesterday," said Seraphious, "And Verrick before her, and Illyan before him—"

"Yes, and?" Fildahorr said.

"I suppose it's my turn," Seraphious told him.

Fildahorr held his head a little higher, regarding his

friend with curious, almost suspicious eyes.

"They asked me to speak to you, many of them, not just the ones who have spoken to you," Seraphious replied, "And I myself share much of their concern—"

"We have to be strong," Fildahorr replied. "We can't let our own homesickness compromise our work here."

"There are hundreds of us, Fildahorr, and it's *rare* we have to defend the Gate from anything. We patrol the Tress day and night and for what? We've seen maybe eight hundred mortals—"

"Closer to a thousand—"

"—in the *full millennium* we've been here. They don't come this far into the woods. There's no point in working so hard all the time and with so many. There's no reason we couldn't take turns, send perhaps twenty back for a few weeks at a time, trade off. No harm would be done—"

"We would lose valuable numbers. Besides, there is nothing left for us in Etheria. All our families, possessions, everything is here, and this Den that the Eredar built for us is far better than any of the ones we'd constructed on our own."

"You cannot tell me you do not miss Etheria," said Seraphious.

"I do. Very much—"

"I suppose it's easier for *you*. You get to return every few months to make your reports—"

"Only for a few hours—"

"It's still *something*," growled Seraphious, "A glimpse, a breath of the air. We're so *close* to it. It's torture being so near the Gate and being told we can't go through."

"Lu`corian charged us with staying here and defending it."

"But he didn't *banish* us here!" Seraphious protested. "Nor has his heir, Siratrian. He didn't say anything at all about all of us needing to be here every moment of every day. *You* have banished us, Fildahorr!"

"I am simply keeping my promise," the Guardian replied.

Seraphious looked at him, seeing no sympathy in his friend. He sighed and got to his feet.

"You should be mindful, Fildahorr," he said, "Or you will make it so that we don't want to guard it at all."

Seraphious rose and stormed out, almost running into Manea in the hallway.

"Seraphious?" she said, seeing he was upset, "What is the matter?"

"You should speak to your mate," he growled, nodding back toward Fildahorr's door, "He takes his work much too seriously."

"You think I don't know that?" said Manea with a fond smile.

"He won't listen," Seraphious told her, "We are unhappy, many of us, and that means nothing to him!"

"It means more than you think." She nudged against him with an encouraging smile. "Just give him a little time—"

"I've given him a thousand years of my time and he's only gotten worse," Seraphious growled. He shoved past her and stormed out of the Den.

Chapter Twenty-Five

When Salazar awoke the next day, it was close to noon. The warauls hadn't woken him for breakfast, as word of his exploits in the night had spread like wildfire through the Den. He went down to the kitchen to find something to silence his growling stomach, then went back to his room, heading straight for the bookshelf to grab the book Fildahorr had given him on the Somadàrsath. It was a thick book and Salazar had only gotten through the first few members recorded in it (although Lu`corian took up a good third of the book by himself). Curious, he opened to the table of contents, skimming down until he stopped at the fifth name, just above Lask's, that read: *Malachi*.

Salazar hesitated, not entirely sure he wanted to know. Scoarin's reaction the previous night told him that Malachi was still living and Scoarin obviously despised the thought of seeing him again. Lask had never even spoken the name of Malachi around his son. Curious and unable to resist the temptation, Salazar turned to the appropriate page and began skimming, words of the chapter sticking in his mind,

Malachi, son of Luke and elder brother of Lask... heir apparent of the Somadar... A man without honor. After the destruction of Hydrellia, he wounded and abandoned his younger brother, leaving the boy to die... He chose the life of a commoner, never taking up his father's sword, abandoning his obligation to the kingdom in its time of need and leaving the land in chaos... After Lask's ascension to power, Malachi plotted to kill him... His attempted murder resulted in the death of the High King Sendanten... Acting with the temporary power of the High King, Lask Somadar disregarded the call for his brother's death, instead casting him out of Etheria forever, banishing him to the mortal world of Earth, where he lives in exile in the Great Forest of Kwynn, where the Moranters and the Warauls ensure he will never return.

Salazar sat there with the book in his lap, stunned. He had an uncle, one who was likely only a few miles away. *That* was why the Warauls forbade him to go westward. *That* was who the Moranters watched for. Salazar was torn between curiosity and resentment. He knew well the story of his father's youth; how Lask had survived Vortearigan's attack on Hydrellia, had watched both of his parents die, and then fled into the Carthonian where he was taken in by the dragon Navar. Salazar realized his father had never told him the full story, how his elder brother had left him.

Salazar found himself disgusted with his uncle, unable to understand how anyone could be so cruel to his own kin, let alone murder his king and abandon Etheria. The boy paused. Apparently he looked a lot like Malachi, and Malachi had never intended to kill the *king*, an accident that led to his banishment. Salazar snapped the book shut, unwilling to admit he had anything in common such a wicked man.

Chapter Twenty-Six

The following day, Salazar heard the howl echo down through the hall from outside. Curious, he made his way toward the steps, and as he did so, he heard a familiar voice from out in the clearing. He stopped short, not believing he had heard it, but then the voice came again and the boy took the steps two at a time and burst up into the clearing, looking for the source. Sure enough, he caught sight of the familiar dark shape of Theramancer and his father, who was sliding from the saddle. Behind him came Myranda.

Salazar was over to them in the blink of an eye and he flung himself at his mother. Myranda clutched him to her and Salazar could hear her breath beside his ear, though he did not know if she laughed or cried.

"I missed you so much, my son," she said, wrapping her fingers in his hair. She pulled back and looked him up and down, studying him from head to toe. "Goodness, it feels like you've grown a foot since I saw you last. Are you alright? They're taking care of you? Feeding you? Are you—?"

"I'm fine, Mother," said Salazar with a smile. "What are you doing here?"

"I just had to see you," Myranda answered. She cupped his face in her hands. "You're father's so good to me. He made up an excuse for us to get away from Letiana for a few days so we could come see you."

Salazar looked back at his father and freed himself from his mother to wrap himself in his father's arms for a moment.

"It is good to see you, my son," Lask said, holding the boy tight to him. "I have missed you terribly."

"I'm sorry for everything, Adar," Salazar murmured into his chest. "I'll never insult Etheria again. You were right about all of it."

Lask wasn't entirely sure what to make of the boy's words, but Salazar was continuing,

"Scoarin said—"

"Scoarin?" Lask echoed. "When did you meet Scoarin? Was she here?"

Salazar realized he had been about to tell his father all about what he had seen, the fact of his disobedience forgotten amid his excitement.

"Salazar?"

Salazar pulled back a bit and Lask found himself

looking down at that all-too-familiar guilty grin.

"What did you do?" he asked.

"It was only for a few hours," said the boy, suddenly regretting his excitement. "And Scoarin was with me."

"I need to have a word with Fildahorr," Lask said, releasing him. "Why don't you show your mother where you've been staying?"

Salazar had expected him to be furious, but instead, Lask simply strode off toward the Den and descended the stairs, heading for the Guardian's chambers. Salazar waited a moment, then he and Myranda went inside as well.

Chapter Twenty-Seven

"Come in," Fildahorr called in reply to the knock on the door. The Guardian's eyes widened and he was instantly on his feet. "Somadar," he said, startled. "What brings you here to the Gate?"

"Myranda needed to see our son," Lask replied, "As did I, though now I find myself needing to see *you*. Would you care to tell me why my son has apparently been in Etheria for several hours when I specifically asked that you not let him go there?"

Horrific guilt played across Fildahorr's features.

"It was an accident, sir—"

"An accident?" Lask echoed.

"Well not so much an accident, as well— he tricked the guards, you see. I didn't know until it was too late—"

"Am I to understand that hundreds of warauls, all of whom are centuries or millennia old, cannot guard the single most important thing in the entire world from a thirteen-year-old boy?"

"He's not just any thirteen-year-old boy, sir," said Fildahorr, the fierce waraul quailed under those fiercer scarlet eyes, "Normally someone would not get that close to the Gate, but he lives here. I trusted him."

"And when were you intending to tell me about this breach of your security?" Lask inquired.

Fildahorr's ears drooped a bit.

"Or *were* you going to tell me?"

"There was no harm done," said the waraul. "He was with Scoarin the whole time and I spoke to him quite sternly about it when he returned—"

"He is my *son*, Fildahorr, my *only* child and heir. *Everything* he does is my concern," Lask growled. "And if I start hearing that this is *not* the only breach like this that you've tried to keep from me, you may force me to move him elsewhere and start reconsidering the Warauls as Gate Guardians."

"I am terribly sorry, Somadar," Fildahorr said, bowing his head. "I have only ever lived to faithfully obey Lu`corian's orders to guard the Gate, and I shall make sure I do not fail again."

Lask lay a hand on the waraul's head.

"I trust you, my friend," he said. "Salazar is a handful, and no one knows that better than I."

Chapter Twenty-Eight

Four Years Later

When Seraphious returned from hunting that afternoon, he found a group of about twenty warauls waiting at his den.

"What is this?" he asked.

"We need to talk, Seraphious," said Verrick. "Most of the others agree, but we decided to keep the group small."

Seraphious glanced over the assembled warauls and found himself wondering how many others were eavesdropping from the thick brush. He leapt up onto the nearby boulder and settled back on his haunches.

"Then speak," he said.

"We want to know what you're waiting for," Verrick replied. "It was almost five hundred years ago that you left the Tress, and since then we have divided Fildahorr's numbers almost in half. We could give a good challenge to the Guardians." He paused. "We are tired of waiting, of living like wolves in the dirt in this godforsaken place. We want to go back to Etheria. That was the promise you made us. We can fight our way through now—"

"And what of the human with them?" asked Seraphious, "The heir of the Somadar? You told me yourself not long ago that he was mastering the magic in his blood. Is that magic *you* want to openly challenge? A few more years and he will be gone—"

"In a few more years we may have starved!" shouted another waraul, Yvana, from down below.

There was a murmur of agreement.

"The Guardians will not surrender the Gate easily," Seraphious replied. "What if they should call the Moranters to their aid? We shall be sorely outnumbered then."

"So you propose we wait even longer until we can outnumber both the remaining Guardians *and* the Moranters?" demanded another. "We'll never get home at that rate!"

Seraphious looked down at the group, at the angry faces glaring up at him. It was the slow-simmering anger of rebellion, anger Seraphious knew well, and he knew it was dangerous. Cold and hunger had hardened these warauls, and he did not question they could and would mutiny unless something was done.

"We can act if you insist, but I have tried to keep it so

that we act within our honor—"

"You lost any honor you had the day you killed Manea!" snapped Yvana.

Seraphious snarled, only to receive a chorus of growls in return.

"Fine!" he growled, "If you wish to return to Etheria as outlaws, to have to live in hiding there, so be it!"

"Even in hiding, at least we'd be home," said Verrick.

"We can't just make an attack on the Gate," Seraphious told them.

"But—"

"We have to draw out Fildahorr's warauls to where they are more manageable and until they are spread so thin we can charge the clearing and be through the Gate before they can mount a proper defense."

"Why would Fildahorr start looking for us now? He raged through these woods at the beginning, but we hid so well, and with all the fighting they exhausted themselves. He's been ignoring us for years."

"We have to force his hand, prove ourselves dangerous, make it so he has no choice but to come for us."

"And how do you propose to do that?" asked Verrick.

"We go after the boy."

Chapter Twenty-Nine

Salazar was walking with quick, long strides, knowing he was already late. He had gone out to take Azarak some breakfast, but the waraul was at a distant post outside of the Tress and the young man had taken a seat there with him while he ate. It wasn't until the sun was already high that he realized he was going to be late.

Fildahorr kept a tight schedule among the warauls, and Salazar was not exempt from it. Every morning, he and the Guardian would take two hours for study. If Salazar had learned anything, it was to never be late where Fildahorr was concerned. Glancing up at the sun through the trees, he knew he already was.

He spotted a pair of warauls running through the trees ahead of him. He assumed Fildahorr had probably sent them out looking for him, and it wasn't until they drew nearer, that Salazar realized he did not recognize either of them.

Just then, three more came charging in from the left, and when Salazar turned to run, he found he had been silently surrounded. There were a dozen of them, fur bristling as they encircled him, snarling and glaring at him through narrowed eyes. The young man reached for his knife.

"I wouldn't do that if I were you," growled the largest of the warauls, a tall golden brown male. "Do you know who I am?"

"No," Salazar lied. Though he guessed immediately who the waraul was, he did not want to give Seraphious the pleasure of having a reputation.

"Then Fildahorr is even more foolish than I thought, keeping you ignorant of my presence. I am Seraphious."

"What do you want?" asked Salazar. He stood still, balanced, hoping the warauls couldn't hear his heart pounding.

"You're in luck, boy," Seraphious said, "If it were not for your illustrious parentage, I would kill you where you stand. As it is, I believe you will be far more useful if I leave you alive."

"How generous of you," Salazar muttered.

Seraphious eyed him with a disdainful gaze.

"You will deliver a message," the waraul continued, "And tell Fildahorr the hour of his defeat draws near. We shall prove him to be the incompetent, arrogant fool that he is and leave him to rot in this wasteland in ruin while we return to our rightful home." His ears laid back as he hissed, "And don't forget the most important part."

Salazar waited to see what that would be, when all of a sudden, Seraphious sprung at him, a thick paw swiping out, claws shredding though his shirt and into his skin. Salazar doubled over, stumbling to his hands and knees. He struggled for his knife, but Seraphious had stepped back to a safe distance, while the other warauls gave a satisfied laugh.

"Best watch yourself, boy," hissed Seraphious, "This forest is going to be a battlefield."

With that, they were gone, disappeared back into the trees as quickly as they had come. Salazar stayed there on his hands and knees, every breath sending a sharp pain across him. He brought a hand up to his stomach, feeling hot blood under his fingers. The young man forced himself to his feet with a grunt and looked down. Four long gashes sliced down his side and across his navel. Salazar knew they were deep and so started off, knowing he did have much time to get within earshot of the Tress before he risked losing too much blood. He staggered on, clutching at the tatters of his shirt, feeling blood trickling through his fingers and down over his waist.

Each step was painful, and he didn't get very far before the throbbing, burning, agony across his midsection forced him back down to his knees. Gasping, he started to crawl, blood spattering the decaying leaves beneath him. He shuffled through the trees on all fours, dirt clinging to his blood soaked fingers. It was difficult to breathe, and black spots began to infringe on the corners of his vision. His head started to swim, the dizziness making him clumsy. It wasn't long until he felt the strength leaving his arms, and managed to flop out onto his back so not to fall on his wounds.

He tried to call for the warauls, but his voice came out as a hoarse croak. He swallowed and coughed, then took a breath. It hurt to shout, but shout he did, calling for help from anyone who could hear him, but no one came. As he lay there, blinking against the blurriness of his vision, Salazar found himself thinking the warauls might not answer a human cry. He took another breath and tilted his head back in the leaves, letting out forlorn waraul-like howl. He coughed and gasped in another breath to try again, but the cry came quieter as his strength left him.

There was a movement off to the right and Salazar blinked, squinting to make out the dark form of Avamor running over a rise in the distance. Blair was close behind him.

"Salazar!" Avamor yelped, "What—?"

"Seraphious," Salazar groaned.

"Get branches," said Blair.

The two warauls combed the forest nearby, finding two long, fallen fir branches. Salazar shifted onto them, feeling the warauls bracing themselves against him to help him move. Once he was there, the young man held on to the branches as best he could, while Blair and Avamor went up to the front, each taking a branch in their mouth. They dug their feet in, dragging him away through the trees back toward the Den.

Salazar closed his eyes, hearing them shuffling through the leaves, no longer stealthy with the work of his weight. He could hear barks in the distance, and Avamor shouted,

"Get Fildahorr!"

Salazar could hear many paws shuffling around him, but the sound soon faded away as he slipped under the dark shade of unconsciousness.

Chapter Thirty

Manea pushed the door open and trotted inside, drawing Fildahorr's eyes up out of his book. He looked up at her, smiling at the sight of her round belly.

"Here," she said, pushing in close to him.

Fildahorr rubbed his face in against her side and suddenly felt a movement there, the shifting of one of the pups she carried. He let out a surprised laugh and nuzzled his face into her fur, saying,

"Why hello there, little one."

Manea smiled.

"He's a restless one," she said. "Takes after you for sure."

Fildahorr grinned. Suddenly, there came barking from outside, the frantic howl of an alarm. The Guardian exchanged a concerned glance with his mate and then rose, going out into the hallway. Manea followed him, worried, as Fildahorr trotted up the steps, and stopped short at the top, stunned and confused by what he saw.

The clearing was divided in two. A group of about one hundred warauls stood snarling in front of the rest, who were lined up before the Gate, blocking the way.

"What is this?" Fildahorr demanded, striding between them.

"They're trying to get through," Seppish growled behind him.

"We just want to go home!" barked Yvana.

Fildahorr stood before the one who led them, saying,

"You would do this? My friend, who is practically my brother, would betray us? Please, we can think of something—"

"You didn't want to hear it," Seraphious growled, "And we are all tired of waiting and tired of treating you like a king. It was never this way in Etheria. We were a community, not a monarchy. We decided things together. We didn't have to take orders, especially not from *you*. Just because you were the favorite of Lu`corian does not make you any better than any of us."

There were howls of approval from behind him.

"Stand aside," Seraphious continued, "Let us pass and we will trouble you no more. We will accept the kingdom's ire if we must. I shall go to the castle—"

"And do what?" Fildahorr demanded. "There is no Somadar now! He lies dead in the ruins of Hydrellia! The kingdom has been brought to its knees. What if Vortearigan should come here? What if he should come through to hide on Earth until his army is strong enough to attack again? The kingdom is in enough trouble as it is, it needs no more problems from you."

"We don't want any trouble. Just let us pass and we will make our own way."

"I cannot let you."

"*Why*?"

"Because we promised! We—"

"*You* promised!" Seraphious snapped. "You took it upon yourself—"

"We *all* chose this!" Fildahorr barked back. "Nothing was forced on us. We decided as a group, came here willingly—"

"And then you had your kingdom! You were supposed to be the overseer, not a jailor! You have made yourself king of us and without our permission!"

There was more barking behind him.

"Let us through," Seraphious growled, "Or name yourself a tyrant."

Fildahorr stood there for a moment, not knowing what to do. He heard Manea snarl from behind him, and a low growl from Seppish and the others, showing well their opinion of Seraphious.

"Seraphious," said Fildahorr, "Please. We can't. We

promised—"

Seraphious lunged at him then, teeth bared. Startled, Fildahorr yelped as Seraphious tackled him, the two kicking and snapping. Barking erupted from both sides and warauls crowded in, shouting,

"Stop! This is not—"

"Kill the traitor!"

"Show him, Seraphious!"

"Kill him!"

"Enough! We are all brothers! This isn't—"

"Get off him!" It was Manea. She smacked Seraphious across the face with a paw, claws raking down the side of his face. Seraphious reared back with howl, lashing out blindly on instinct.

There was a chorus of gasps and the scene froze, deathly silent. Manea collapsed into the leaves, gasping and gurgling, unable to breathe from where Seraphious's claws had found their mark on her throat. She thrashed, clumsy with her swollen belly, and Fildahorr was there in an instant, screaming,

"MANEA!"

She choked and sputtered, looking up at him with wide eyes, then lay a paw over his, her struggles calming.

"No!" Fildahorr barked. "No, please!"

Seraphious looked on, horrified, seeing Manea fading before his eyes, and taking her unborn pups with her.

She could not even speak to tell her mate goodbye. Fildahorr rubbed his face over hers, whispering frantic, begging words into her ears, but to no avail. She heaved a blood spattered sigh over his feet and her breath came no more.

There was a stunned silence hanging over all the warauls who stood by, aghast, as Fildahorr rose, shaking. When he turned his gaze up from his mate, his wrathful eyes fell squarely on Seraphious. He roared, harsh voice echoing off the trees,

"I'll send you to *Hell* before I send you home!"

He lunged at him, but Seraphious didn't have the heart to fight him. Fildahorr's claws sank into his shoulder, but Seraphious struggled free of him. The warauls with him had turned and were tearing out of the clearing. Seraphious joined them, Fildahorr hard on his heels. The other guardians charged after them, howling, forcing them out of the clearing, pursuing them into the woods, driving them to the very edge of the Tress.

"Traitor!" Fildahorr was roaring. "Set foot here again and I shall destroy you!" The betrayer was gone, disappeared into the trees with his rabble, but still Fildahorr was shrieking, "Hide yourself well, traitor! I shall search every hill and vale for you and if I should find you, I will bring upon you such a vengeance that you will *beg* for Hell's fury instead!"

Chapter Thirty-One

It was warm, and would have been comfortable if not for the throbbing across his midsection. As Salazar came to, he realized there was something warm and wet lapping at his side and when he opened his eyes, he realized it was a waraul's tongue.

"Oh God, Fildahorr!" he groaned, pushing at the waraul's head with a weak a hand, disgusted.

"Stay still," said the Guardian, bowing his head again.

"Don't—"

"I don't know what you expect me to do," said Fildahorr, looking down at him. The waraul's muzzle was stained red in Salazar's blood. "No one here has hands and we must tend your wounds."

Salazar found himself in Fildahorr's room and noticed Seppish was there as well, sitting off to the side, chewing. The waraul was taking up mouthfuls of herbs, chewing them up, then spitting them into a bowl. Salazar knew exactly what they were for and groaned,

"No, don't even think about putting that on me. That is not—"

"It must be done," Fildahorr told him. "Our spit is clean and will prevent infection. Now lay still so we can finish."

Salazar settled back and stared up at the ceiling, disgusted. He suddenly found himself very homesick, wishing for his familiar bed where human hands could tend him. He closed his eyes and tried not to think about it when Seppish came over and began licking the poultice into his wounds.

Fildahorr went over and rinsed his mouth in a bucket of water then came to sit by Salazar's head while Seppish worked.

"Avamor tells me Seraphious did this," said the Guardian.

"Yes," Salazar replied.

"Where were you when it happened?"

"Coming back from visiting Azarak, probably only a half mile out from the Tress perimeter."

Fildahorr gave a low, rumbling growl.

"Why did he attack you?" asked the waraul. "Did he say?"

"He said he plans to make the forest a battlefield, that he intends to shame you and return to Etheria."

"Unlikely," Fildahorr growled. "From now on, I don't want you going outside the Tress. It is no longer safe." He bowed his head to nudge Salazar's, nuzzling at his dark hair as if he were a puppy. "Try to sleep. You need to rest."

Chapter Thirty-Two

When Salazar awoke later in the afternoon, he was aware of a pounding in his head. He put a hand over his eyes allowing them to get adjusted to the light before opening them again, looking around, blinking. There was no one else in the room, and he looked down to where the warauls had treated his wounds. They had bandaged him as best they could, but they hadn't been able to do a very good job of it, so Salazar retied the bandages around himself, having to shift a bit to position them. He grunted, feeling the pain flare across him again, but tried not think about it, letting his fingers tie the bandages before he lay back again, feeling exhausted.

He was aware of how empty the room felt and glanced toward the door, imagining how comforting it would be to see his mother appear through it with a bowl of her chicken stew and fresh bread, or his father come in with some foul-smelling liquid, but one that was sure to ease the pain.

Salazar was not often homesick in the Den, as he had come to think of the Warauls as his family, but lying there wounded, he felt a cold aching for human company. He propped himself up a bit and shifted back so he could sit up, leaning against the wall. His wounds twinged with the movement, and he put a hand to his stomach on reflex. Pushing the pain aside, he leaned over and grabbed the water bucket, pulling it over into his lap with a grimace. He sat there for a moment, taking a breath, then pulled the medallion out of his shirt.

It had been a while since he had tried to scry anything, but the young man remembered what he had done before. He closed his eyes, summoning up the magic. The light in the room flared a bit brighter, seeming to gather around him. Taking a hold on it with his mind, he cast it down into the bucket, until the water glowed. Opening his eyes, he asked of the water,

"Show me my home."

The water rippled and the light twisted and writhed, forming into the shape of tall trees and golden leaves that glistened in the wind.

"No, my home *here*," he said, "Here, with my family."

The light rippled again, shifting into the shape of the familiar house in Letiana. The vision took him inside to where his mother was clipping flower stems at the counter to arrange them in a vase for the table. The simple scene made Salazar realize just how much he missed her.

Another figure appeared, the light twisting around him as he came in from the side of the vision. It was his father. He looked tired, weary in all senses of the term, as he set down a stack of letters on the table to be sent. He went over to the counter, wrapping his arms around Myranda's waist from behind her and put his head on her shoulder, seeming to take a bit of comfort in being near her and the sight of the flowers she worked with. Myranda gave him a sympathetic look, reaching back to brush a hand against his face. She said something, but Salazar did not have the energy to make the vision carry her voice. Lask shook his head and Myranda looked disappointed, but resigned.

"What are you doing?"

Salazar started and looked up to see Fildahorr standing in the door, wearing a very dissatisfied expression. The magic dissipated immediately and Salazar set the bucket aside, looking back to the waraul with guilty eyes.

"You need to be resting," said the Guardian. "Magic will sap your energy and you need all the energy you have to heal." Fildahorr glanced from the bucket to the young man. "Scrying?"

Salazar's guilty look was all the answer he needed.

"Your family?" Fildahorr guessed.

Salazar nodded. Fildahorr padded over and settled down next to him, curling his warm, furry side against the young man. Salazar put an arm over his back, glad for the company, even if it was waraul and not human.

"You'll be out of here before long," said Fildahorr.

"Three more years."

"One day, when you're a thousand years old, three years won't seem so bad."

Chapter Thirty-Three

The next day, Fildahorr still would not let Salazar leave the room. Salazar protested, as his wounds were well scabbed over and getting smaller by the hour, but the waraul would not relent. The young man stayed in the Guardian's chambers, reading for part of the morning until he got bored.

He reached over and took up the medallion that lay on the floor beside him to entertain himself. He reached out with his mind and got a hold on the gold light that illuminated the room. He pulled it together into a ball in the center of the room, hovering over the floor, making the rest of the room darker.

Salazar pulled at the light with his mind, his hands working through the air as he divided the light in half, forming it into a glowing dragon. He set it aside and formed another with the remaining light, then made them soar around the room, flapping their shining wings with lazy strokes. He made the two come together and play in the air; locking talons, diving down to the floor, sending bouts of gold fire up to the ceiling.

It was pleasant watching the light dragons play. He had them diving, rolling, and looping. He didn't know how long he lay there admiring them, but suddenly the door opened.

"Hey!" Azarak exclaimed in glee, bounding into the room.

Salazar started in surprise and the dragons dispersed, the light filling back out into the room.

"Azarak!" he exclaimed, his heart nigh having leapt out of his chest.

"Do it again!" barked Azarak, wagging his tail and nodding with excitement.

Reluctant this time, Salazar called the light back together and made the dragons reappear. Azarak watched, enthralled as they soared about the room. Salazar glanced over at him with a mischievous grin and he sent one of the light dragons diving down on the waraul, sending a jet of gold flame out on his backside. Azarak yelped.

Salazar snickered and let the dragons disappear again.

"It's *not* funny!" Azarak cried. "I think you've burnt my hindquarters!"

He went over to one of the pillows and sat down,

dragging his backside across it, whimpering.

"Azarak! Fildahorr sleeps on that!"

"Then don't tell him!" Azarak retorted, still rubbing his singed rump across the cushion.

Salazar shook his head.

It was at that moment the Guardian of the Tress entered the room.

There was a stunned, awkward silence. Salazar still lay on the pillow, Azarak was frozen in mid rump-drag on the cushion and Fildahorr stood in the doorway with a look of shocked disgust written over his features.

"Azarak!" he barked.

"It's not what it looks like," Azarak said.

"Yes it is," Salazar laughed

"Hush up," Azarak hissed out the corner of his mouth.

"Get up," Fildahorr said, padding over to the other waraul, "Up!"

"But he singed me!" Azarak cried. To prove his point, he promptly raised his tail and showed the Guardian his reddened backside.

"Get out!" Fildahorr barked. "*OUT*!"

"Alright," Azarak yipped. "I'm going!"

As he passed, Fildahorr gave the waraul a swift kick in the already hurting backside, was rewarded by a loud yelp, then shut the door. Salazar could not help but laugh.

Fildahorr went over and inspected his bed, then flopped down on the floor instead.

"Sorry," said Salazar, "I suppose that *was* sort of my fault."

Fildahorr cast a glance at him from the corner of his eye.

"I was thinking," Salazar said, changing the subject, "That maybe once I've healed, we should tell the Moranters about Seraphious. I could go with you; I've never met them—"

"They've already been told," the Guardian replied. "I sent Seppish to inform them yesterday."

Salazar didn't bother to hide his disappointment.

"Besides," Fildahorr continued, "I don't want you setting foot outside of the Tress from now on. It isn't safe—"

"So I'm to be a prisoner now?" Salazar protested.

"The Tress is large, boy. You should have plenty of space."

Salazar knew that a one-mile radius around the Gate was a decent sized area, but nonetheless, the idea of being confined didn't sit well with him.

Chapter Thirty-Four

When Fildahorr was at last satisfied Salazar was healed, the young man was allowed back outside. Having been a prisoner in the Den for the past two days, Salazar was all too eager to get out into the open air. He wandered the clearing for a while and took a short walk that morning, but he soon felt the confines of the Tress pressing in on him. It was a strange thing, as he often stayed within its bounds anyway, but having been *ordered* to do so left him with a new, indignant feeling, one that nagged at him as the morning went on. Was he to be a prisoner of so small an area for the next three years? Salazar wasn't about to let Fildahorr do that to him.

He assured the guards he was just going out to visit Azarak at his post on the perimeter of the Tress, but as soon as he was out of sight of the brush wall, he turned his course west, heading slightly north out of the Tress.

He knew he probably shouldn't be wandering out this far by himself, but Salazar had nothing better to do and there was nothing like boredom to drive a young man to mischief. He kept a hand on his knife, wary of his surroundings, and took a winding route through the trees to the northwest as the sun peaked higher toward noon and passed it.

It was cold that afternoon, and seemed to be getting colder, although Salazar could see no discernible change in the weather. He picked his way through the trees, when all of a sudden, he noticed a large insect fluttering between the trunks ahead of him.

It was a luna moth. Salazar blinked, thinking his eyes must be tricking him, for it was far too cold for a moth to be out, nor had he ever seen a luna moth before. They were not found in Letiana or Kwynn, or anywhere on Earth that Salazar knew of. The only picture he had ever seen of one had been in one of his father's Etherian books. The presence of the moth made him both wary and intrigued.

The moth landed on a tree just ahead of him, fanning its wings for a moment before fluttering off into the trees. Salazar watched it go, not knowing what to make of it. He shook his head, then continued on the way he had been going. It wasn't long until he felt the cold creeping up on his heels. That was when he caught sight of something from the corner of his eye.

His gaze snapped over to the place, but there was nothing there. Salazar glanced around at the surrounding trees, feeling a chill prickle up his spine. Thinking it was better to be paranoid than hurt again, he drew his knife before he turned to continue on the way he had been going, but started and stopped short.

There was man standing there just ahead of him. Entirely white, his garb, his skin, his hair was the color of the frost on the leaves. The only bit of color on him was the sharp, bright scarlet of his eyes. He raised a hand to place a single finger against his lips, his gaze never wavering nor blinking from where it held the young man fixed.

Salazar stood there, awed, terrified, and bewildered. By all descriptions, this was Lu`corian, the second of the First, his two millennia dead great-great-grandfather. The spirit's presence made him feel tiny; the same sort of wondering insignificance he had felt when standing under the heavens of Etheria. The young man could only stand there, gaping, and it seemed as though he blinked and the figure was gone.

Salazar looked around, startled, then all of a sudden, caught sight of him again, farther away among the trees. Intrigued, despite his fear, the young man sheathed his knife and went after him, weaving around the trees. Lu`corian stood there, hands clasped behind his back, waiting until Salazar drew near, then disappeared again.

"Hey!" Salazar exclaimed.

He caught sight of the figure again, farther away, back turned to him. Salazar went after him, calling,

"Wait! What—?"

The spirit whirled back to him, ghostly cloak flaring in an unfelt wind, snapping a long finger back up to his lips with an angry and urgent expression. Salazar bit back any further words and hurried after him. Again, Lu`corian disappeared as he approached, only to reappear through the trees, leading him along no path that Salazar could see.

Just as he caught up, the spirit disappeared again, and Salazar looked all around, but did not see him.

"Great," he muttered, knowing he'd let himself get lost in an unfamiliar part of the forest.

He turned in a complete circle, scanning the trees, but there was no sign of the ghost. Glancing down, Salazar caught sight of a set of tracks in the leaves. They were large, longer than Salazar's foot, and broad, with long toes that ended in deep furrows that could only be made by formidable claws. There was a swaying line that wound between them; the drag mark from a tail. Salazar guessed they must be moranter tracks. Seeing the spirit did not intend to appear again, Salazar decided he had no better option than to follow the tracks. If nothing else, perhaps they would lead him somewhere familiar. He followed the trail through the trees, just a little ways, until he saw the woods thin out into a small clearing.

Salazar peered through the trees, not knowing what to make of what he saw there. It was a cottage— no, perhaps a cabin. It was very small and he guessed there would only be about two rooms inside, or one large one. The style of it was strange. Though it was a tiny place, the roof came to a sharp peak, and there was a sort of porch on the front, though it was level with the ground. There were four pillars supporting the porch (or *overhang*, Salazar thought might be more appropriate), and each one was so intricately carved, there was not a single surface that did not host some carving, just like the solid, triangular front of the overhang. Even the door was made of carved panels.

Salazar could not imagine just how long it would have taken to complete that much tedious woodwork. There were more sets of moranter tracks weaving around the trees and out in the clearing itself. Glancing around, he saw no movement in the clearing or through the open windows of the place, so guessed the owner was not at home. He crept out closer to the cabin, intrigued, wanting to get a closer look at it.

There were carvings of dragons, griffins, centaurs, waraculs, moranters, trees and blossoms, and they were so accurate, Salazar knew their craftsman could have only been Etherian. He laid a pale hand on one of the pillars over one of the griffins there, feeling the delicate ridges of each carved feather.

He looked through the open window at the front and saw the inside was packed full of equally extravagant furniture, hardly befitting such a small, isolated place. The carved decorations on the furniture looked to be the same work of whoever had carved the exterior. The bed at the back was unmade and had such ragged linens, Salazar wondered why someone with such obvious skill could not afford better cloth.

There was the crack of a stick breaking from in the woods nearby, so Salazar bolted back into the trees like a rabbit, not wanting to be seen snooping. He was so absorbed in thinking about the strange place he had seen and getting away from whoever might be following him, he did not see the warauls until they were right on top of him.

There were two of them, and Salazar realized, too late, that they were unfamiliar. One of them took a flying leap, front paws smacking into his chest and shoving him over backward to pin him there in the leaves. Salazar was scrambling for his knife, seeing the snarling face just inches from his own, but the waraul pulled back, looking down at him as if confused.

Salazar had worked his knife loose and, unlike his attacker, he did not hesitate. He stabbed the waraul in the side and the creature leapt back with a high yelp. The other lunged for the young man with a snarl and Salazar did not have time to get up, but he didn't need to.

The charging waraul came to an abrupt halt and fell onto its side, an arrow sticking out of its forehead. There was the whizzing of fletching as another came flying in, finding its mark in the wounded waraul's skull, making quick work of the pair.

Salazar scrambled to his feet and whirled, brandishing his knife, not knowing if he would be the next target. His mouth dropped open.

It was like seeing an older manifestation of himself. The man was tall and slender, with tousled black hair and skin as pale as Salazar's. He watched the young man before him with sharp green eyes. There was a piercing fixedness to his gaze, like the way a snake watches an unsuspecting mouse. He resembled Lask, though his face was narrower and his sharp nose was not quite as long. He wore a satisfied, crafty, smirk; an almost sinister look that would never have appeared on Lask's countenance.

"Snooping around, yet not even a hello for your dear old uncle?" hissed the man.

"Malachi," Salazar breathed, stunned.

"You should thank me, boy," he said, pointing the end

of his bow toward the fallen warauls, "The only reason they hesitated was because they thought you were me. If you bore the accursed red eyes of my brother, you would have been dead this day."

He turned and walked away back into the trees, disappearing among them like the specter that had led the young man. Part of Salazar wanted to run after him; there were so many things he could ask him. His other, and more persuasive, side told him to run in the opposite direction, for Malachi was an exiled murderer and all the warauls said never to trust him.

He stared in the direction Malachi had gone, making certain he was not coming back, then turned and jogged away into the forest back the way he had come. Or the way he *thought* he had come; Salazar realized that in following Lu`corian's ghost he had lost all trace of the faint trail he'd been following and now had very little idea of where he was.

He looked skyward, but (of course, curse his luck!) it was cloudy, making it impossible to tell where the sun was in the sky. He stopped and took a breath, trying to sense the direction of the Gate; he could always feel it a bit, the distant presence of Etheria, that indefinable pull towards home. Sure enough, the longer he stood there, the more he felt that faint tug in his mind. He turned, starting off toward what must have been southeast.

He made his way through the forest, wary, but without incident, until he found a faint, winding, trail amid the trees. He followed it until he noticed more tracks in the dirt. There were two sets of the tracks, moranter again, one slightly smaller than the other, so Salazar guessed that a pair of the creatures had been walking together. He had just knelt down to inspect the prints, to decide how fresh they were, when he heard a rustle in the leaves off to the side.

Salazar looked over to see the source of the tracks. A pair of moranters were lumbering along nearby. They were longer than Salazar was tall, though stood only perhaps to his waist. They were enormous lizards, though a short mane of silvery hair grew in a line from the top of their head down their neck, and they both had a short silver beard along their chin and throat. One's bumpy skin was dark green; the other was dusty brown. They both looked startled when they caught sight of him.

"Hey!" shouted the green one, gathering his wits. "You are not zuppozed to be here!"

"Get him!" snapped the other.

Salazar was surprised at how fast they could move. The moranters came charging after him, stubby legs flailing in a clumsy, loping run, but one that was shockingly quick. The young man took off running, having to turn west as his pursuers cut off the path back to the Gate.

"Wait!" he called over his shoulder, "Wait! I'm—"

He tripped over something and fell out onto dusty ground. He was scrambling to get up when he realized he had emerged into a clearing and there were about fifty pairs of lizard-like eyes looking at him in surprise. Moranters had poked their heads out of their burrows at the commotion or looked up from their places resting in the leaves. Salazar hardly got a chance to look at them, since the two came charging up behind him at the same time that an enormous brown one came bursting up out of a burrow near the perimeter.

The newcomer was on him before Salazar could even get to his feet, and the young man found himself pinned against the ground by a heavy clawed foot. He looked up into a brown face and a snarling mouthful of pointed teeth. Two narrowed amber eyes glared down at him.

"How dare you zhow your faze here?" the creature snarled. "Murderer!"

"It was an accident," Salazar replied, wondering how the Moranters knew about his crime.

"Zo you've zaid," growled the moranter. His amber eyes glanced back to the other two who had chased the young man into the clearing. "You two loutz drag him back to ze cottage and give him a reminder to ztay away."

The other two exchanged eager grins.

"Wait!" Salazar yelped. "I'm not Malachi—"

"You have had many namez, traitor—"

"I am Salazar Somadàrsath, son of Lask!"

The moranter's eyes narrowed even further and a long forked tongue flicked out just inches from Salazar's face.

"He doez look a bit young to be Malachi," remarked the dark green one.

"Ah don't recall azking *you*, Azir," the moranter growled, then looked back down to Salazar, inspecting him. "If you are not Malachi, zhen what are you doing zo cloze to uz?"

"I just went for a walk—"

"Zhiz far into ze lozt reachez of ze Kwynnizh forezt?"

"I'm staying at the Gate. Surely Fildahorr told you I have been with them?"

"He did." The moranter turned his head so to regard him with a single sharp eye. "Zhough he alzo zaid you were going to be ztaying wizhin ze boundz of ze Trezz now zhat Zeraphiouz haz been zpotted."

"He probably should have mentioned that I also don't listen very well."

The moranter hissed at him, a wave of hot rancid breath washing over Salazar's face.

"Oh for heaven's sake, Kairn!" came a new voice.

Salazar turned his head to see a figure, a *human* figure, pull herself out of a nearby burrow. Stunned, he watched her walk over.

"You just enjoy being a bully. Let him up."

Kairn's snarling face shifted to a more sheepish look for an instant before he looked back down to Salazar under his foot and bared his teeth again.

"He zhould not be wandering zo cloze to uz wizhout an invitation, particularly when Zeraphiouz haz made it clear he meanz him harm. What if—?"

"Well, he's here now," said the girl, "And no amount of fussing is going to change that." She came and leaned her weight against the moranter, making him shift over and pick his foot up from Salazar's chest. "Leave him be. Asmodeus will be back in an hour or so, he can decide about him then."

Kairn gave her a sour look, but nonetheless, turned and lumbered away, slinking back down into his burrow. The other two exchanged glances then sauntered away, unconcerned. Salazar looked up to his rescuer, who was offering a hand to help him up.

She was around his age, with thick curly brown hair, and hazel eyes, with a light sun-kiss of freckles across the bridge of her nose. For a moment he could only lay there, looking up at her.

"Come on," she said, splaying her fingers, impatient.

Salazar took her hand and let her help him to his feet.

"Who are you?" he asked.

"Rhia," she replied.

"You *live* here? With *them*?"

"Yes. Don't let Kairn fool you. He's a pushover really."

Salazar begged to differ. Rhia wandered to the edge of the clearing and Salazar followed close behind her, not wanting to be left alone with the moranters who still milled about the clearing, watching him. She settled down on a stump there and Salazar folded his legs to sit on the ground next to her.

"Are you an Immortal?" she inquired. Salazar noticed her accent was Kwynnish, but one that carried an undertone that echoed the Moranters' thick speech.

"Yes."

"Oh." She looked disappointed. "Then how old are you?"

"Seventeen."

Rhia looked surprised, and considered him with a renewed interest.

"Are you a mortal?" asked Salazar, equally surprised.

"Yes."

"How did you get out here? The Immortals normally don't let any mortals within miles of them."

"I've always been here," said Rhia. "My parents abandoned me out in the wilderness when I was just a baby.

Asmodeus found me and has taken care of me all my life."

Salazar's eyes widened, unable to imagine the fearsome moranters trying to care for a baby.

"You've stayed with them all this time?" he said, amazed.

"Yes. I go into the village outside of the forest from time to time to get things when I need them. Asmodeus or Kairn go with me and watch from the trees. They're very protective." She gave a fond smile. "It wasn't particularly smart to come here by yourself," she remarked. "You do look an awful lot like Malachi, and Kairn hates *him*."

"You've seen him?"

"Only twice, and always from a distance. Asmodeus said to stay away from him. Kairn says he's an exiled murderer."

"So am I, but I'm not that bad."

Rhia gave him a strange look.

"You're a murderer?" she asked, voice quiet.

"Accidentally. It was more in defense than anything— wait, where are you going?"

Rhia had gotten up and backed away from him. She watched him, wary, then disappeared into one of the burrows. Salazar looked after her, disappointed. She was the first girl he'd seen in years, and the only human his own age he'd had contact with in all that time.

He looked out over the clearing. The moranters

seemed to have lost interest in him already, going back to napping in the leaves, or sharing a lunch with each other. They were omnivorous like the warauls, Salazar noticed, as they chewed on acorns and late berries as well as the dismembered rabbit one of them had caught. Apparently they weren't as picky about whether their food was cooked or not.

In time, Salazar saw Kairn emerge from his burrow, lumbering over towards the young man. The moranter settled down in the leaves in front of him, narrowing his eyes.

"Rhia zayz you admit to killing zomeone."

"Yes," Salazar replied, realizing the burrows must be connected underground. "You already knew. I don't see why—"

"You frightened her," Kairn continued, "You are ze firzt hooman zhe haz met who iz her own age, or at leazt, ze only one who iz privy to ze zecretz of ze Immortalz like her. Zhe waz exzited, glad to meet you, but now zhe fearz you. Zhe knowz little about ze world and ze darknezz in it." He tilted his head in closer to the young man's. "Ah don't know how or why you killed zhiz man, but know zhiz, hooman: if you zhould even *zhink* about hurting Rhia, Ah will turn your inzidez out wizh mah clawz and zhred zhem wizh mah teezh, no matter whoze blood iz in your veinz. You may be ze zon of Lazk, but you rezemble Malachi in more wayz zhan one. Zo watch your ztep."

His long, forked tongue flicked out towards Salazar's face, then he rose and lumbered away. Salazar looked after him, wide-eyed, thinking Kairn was the most terrifying beast he had ever come across. Before Kairn could disappear back into the burrow, his head turned and he changed course, lumbering over to the other side of the clearing.

Salazar looked to see another moranter emerging from the trees, just as large as Kairn, with brownish-green skin. The two spoke to each other as they crossed the clearing, and Salazar was able to hear them as they came closer.

"Ah zaw two," said the greenish one, "Zhey are roaming nearer now. Zheze two were frezhly killed wizh arrowz. Malachi'z work, Ah am zure."

"Or Zalazar'z," said Kairn. "Ze hooman haz dizobeyed Fildahorr and haz been wandering about. Zee zhere, Ah have kept him here for you."

Salazar saw the green one's golden eyes look in his direction. In contrast to the scowl on Kairn's face, this moranter's jaws opened in a wide grin.

"Zalazar!" he exclaimed, loping over. "It iz very nize to meet you at lazt. Ah have heard many zhingz about you."

"Oh?" said the young man, glancing back to where Kairn was still glaring at him from a distance.

"Yez, indeed. Ah am Azmodeuz," the moranter continued. "You have already met mah brozher, Kairn."

"I did," Salazar replied with a nervous smile.

"Ah muzt azk, Zalazar," Asmodeus was continuing, "Zurely you did not zhink it wize to be wandering by yourself? And zo zoon after you were attacked?"

"To be honest I was thinking more out of spite," Salazar admitted.

"Zo it waz you, zhen, who zhot zhoze waraulz?"

"No, that was Malachi."

Asmodeus's expression darkened suddenly, and Salazar now saw his resemblance to Kairn.

"Why did you go zhere?" demanded the moranter. "Zhat waz very foolizh. Malachi hatez your fazher and would likely have no compunctionz about hurting you in order to hurt him. You zhould never go zhere again!"

"He saved my life," said Salazar.

Asmodeus looked surprised, but still suspicious.

"Malachi doez not do anyzhing for anyone unlezz it haz zome advantage for him," said the moranter. "Do not expect ze zame kindezz and tezt your luck wizh him again." He paused, considering the young man. "Come. Ah will walk wizh you back to ze Trezz. It iz dangerouz for you to go alone."

Salazar rose and followed the moranter out of the clearing. As they left, Salazar looked over his shoulder and saw Rhia looking up out of one of the burrows, watching him. She blinked large hazel eyes at him, wary, shy, and intrigued all at once, then gave him faint smile.

Chapter Thirty-Five

"Where *have* you been?" Fildahorr was irate. "I've had warauls out scouring the forest for you, half expecting them to find your mauled carcass somewhere! Fool of a boy! Seraphious nearly spills your entrails all over the forest and you think it's a good idea to go for a stroll two days later! And by yourself! Creator in Heaven, Salazar, if you're not going to listen, at least take someone with you!"

"Asmodeus walked back with me."

"So you decided to test your luck with the Moranters, eh? It's a wonder they didn't tear you limb from limb on sight!"

"Rhia kept Kairn from hurting me."

"Rhia," Fildahorr said. "I should have known."

"You knew about her?" Salazar demanded, wondering why Fildahorr had never introduced them.

"Of course I know about her," Fildahorr growled.

"And you're lucky she was there, I'll wager. For someone as intelligent as you, Salazar, you can certainly be so very stupid. Do you *know* what would happen if you were to be killed? Not only would the Somadar be once more without an heir, I would have to explain to him why his only son was gallivanting around by himself after—"

Fildahorr was still talking, but Salazar didn't hear him. His mind had wandered back to the Moranter's clearing where Rhia was smiling that shy, beguiling, smile up at him. Then she was sitting there, in a patch of sunshine, combing her hair. The sun cast her skin in gold as those soft loose curls bounced and sprung—

"Salazar? Salazar, are you even *listening* to me?"

Fildahorr was watching him, leaned forward, furry brows raised, amazed and expectant.

"Not really," Salazar admitted.

Fildahorr sighed and his ears flattened.

"Sorry," murmured Salazar.

"Honestly, boy, what, pray tell, is so occupying in your thoughts that you completely disregard everything that is relevant to your safety?"

"What?"

"Precisely," Fildahorr muttered. He glared at the young man. "Now then, if you *insist* on leaving the Tress, you need to take at least two warauls with you at all times. I'd prefer you not leave the bounds at all, but if you're going to do it anyway, then for heaven's sake, don't sneak off and go alone! Now go get some supper and get to bed, boy. Maybe in the morning your head will be on straight again."

Chapter Thirty-Six

Unfortunately for Fildahorr, when dawn came, Salazar's head was not even close to being on straight. If anything, it had left his shoulders entirely to spend the day in the clouds. As he sat among the warauls at breakfast, he said,

"I think I'll go visit the Moranters again today."

"You mean visit *Rhia*?" teased Azarak.

"Yes," Salazar admitted with a guilty smile. "Want to come?"

Azarak looked over to Fildahorr, who gave Salazar a disappointed look and sighed,

"Take Avamor with you too."

After they had finished, Salazar and his two escorts set off into the woods, following the faint trail westward.

"So that's what's got you all giddy, eh boy?" asked Avamor. "Spotted the Moranters' girl, then?"

"Don't tease him like that," Azarak said with a scolding glance over at him, then grinned, "This is how you do it." He burst out in a singsong voice with, "Salazar loves the lizards' girl—"

Salazar reached down and tugged Azarak's ear, his song breaking off into a yelp. Avamor snickered.

"I just want to see her again, that's all," said the young man. "I've been a bit starved of human company, you know."

"You mean we're not enough for you?" gasped Azarak in mock insult.

Salazar reached for his ear again and Azarak ducked with a sheepish yip.

They approached the Moranters' clearing as the sun was climbing high in the sky and Salazar spotted Azir basking in a patch of sunshine on the perimeter.

"Hello, hooman!" he said. "Ah won't pounze on you zhiz time." He flashed a toothy grin.

"I appreciate it," Salazar replied.

"Lazing away again, eh?" said Azarak trotting over. "Sounds like splendid idea." He settled down beside the moranter, striking up a conversation while Salazar wandered further into the clearing.

Avamor padded over to a small group of moranters on the other side of the clearing, as Salazar approached the burrow where Rhia had disappeared the previous day. He knelt down, inquiring,

"Rhia?"

"Salazar?" She appeared down below, looking surprised to see him.

"We didn't get off to a very good start yesterday, so I thought perhaps we could try again. May I come in?"

She considered him, then nodded, moving to the side so he could climb down. It was larger than he'd anticipated inside, tall enough to allow him to stand comfortably without ducking. It was a dug-out hollow, tamped down on all sides til it was almost hard as stone. There was an alcove dug into one wall that served as a bed, draped in a few fraying linens and a thick bearskin blanket.

Shelves were dug into the walls and hosted all manner of things; colorful rocks and odd shaped pieces of wood. There were elegant lichen clusters and dried bees' nests and long graceful bird feathers. Her dresses were folded on one of the shelves, accompanied by pendants crafted from feathers or stones, likely ones she had made herself. There were a few books also on the shelves next to an opening that Salazar guessed led out into the neighboring burrow.

There were things drawn on the walls in charcoal and Salazar spotted the burned stick that she used for it in the corner. She had decorated the walls with drawings of flora and fauna, moranters, and one of herself. She was not a bad artist, as he could easily distinguish Asmodeus from Kairn, and the different kinds of flowers.

"These are very good," he said, taking them in.

"Thank you," Rhia replied. She pushed herself up to sit on the bed. "They keep me occupied when I get bored."

"Where did these come from?" Salazar inquired, looking over her books.

"I bought a few of them in the village, and Asmodeus brought me the rest from Etheria."

"How do you afford things when you go out of the forest?"

"The moranters keep a bit of Etherian currency. The mortals outside the forest don't seem to mind where the money comes from as long as they get their silver."

Salazar was fascinated. He folded his legs to sit in the floor, resting his back against the wall.

"Haven't you wanted to leave?" he asked. "Be around other humans?"

"I get lonesome sometimes," she admitted, "But I wouldn't want to leave. I like it here. They are my family and Asmodeus is the only father I've ever known."

Just then, there was the sound of shuffling and an all too familiar head poked into the room. Amber eyes fell on Salazar.

"You again," Kairn hissed. "Returning zo zoon? Ah would have zhought yezterday'z eventz would have been enough to keep you away."

"I wanted to visit Rhia," Salazar replied, trying not to let the moranter intimidate him.

Kairn's eyes narrowed.

"Iz he bozhering you?" he asked of Rhia.

"Not yet," Rhia replied with a smile.

"You zhould not be alone wizh him."

"I can take care of myself just fine."

Kairn gave her a skeptical look, then swung his head back towards Salazar.

"Keep your diztanze," he hissed. "Don't even zhink of touching her."

With that, the moranter turned and disappeared back down the tunnel. Rhia smiled a bit when he left, but Salazar was still looking after him, half expecting the enormous lizard to turn around and lunge at him.

"He's just a bit protective is all," Rhia said, "Like any good uncle should be."

"A bit," Salazar echoed.

Rhia looked at him, her eyes scanning him up and down, lingering on his pale hands.

"Why did you want to visit me?" she asked.

The question caught Salazar a little off guard, but he replied,

"After yesterday, I thought I could stand to prove that I'm pretty harmless—"

"You *killed* somebody."

"Not on purpose," he muttered, "That makes a difference."

Rhia eyed him.

"And I haven't been able to talk to other humans very often the past couple of years," he continued, "And I thought maybe you'd like a little company as well." He paused, looking up at her, then admitted, "And you're very pretty."

Rhia blushed and looked away.

"I didn't mean to embarrass you," Salazar said, cursing himself for saying it. There was something about her that made it impossible to hold his tongue.

"I haven't been around humans very much," Rhia told him. "I've never been friends with a human before, and certainly not a male one, and I'm still not sure I want to be. If you want to come visit the Moranters, that's one thing, but you shouldn't come just to see me, especially if you don't know whether or not I want to see *you*."

Salazar felt like a plant deprived of water and thought that the slightest breeze could have blown him over.

"Don't take it so personally," said Rhia, looking guilty when she saw the expression that crossed his face.

Salazar wondered just how he *should* take it.

"I don't know what to think," Rhia continued, trying to explain herself. "You're my age, but Immortal. You have noble blood, but talk to me like a regular person. You killed a man, but want me to think you're harmless."

Salazar sat there, saying nothing. She spoke casually and though there was no venom in her voice, he fancied each word fell on him like a whiplash. He cleared his throat and shifted, getting to his feet saying,

"Sorry. I shouldn't have assumed anything. I won't bother you anymore." He went over to climb back up out of the burrow.

He started back across the clearing toward Azarak, glancing over his shoulder. Rhia was watching him go, resting her chin on arms that were folded on the ground outside of the burrow. He did not know what to make of her. She did not look angry or pleased to see him leave, but rather just watched him with a sort of shy curiosity. She didn't smile at him again.

"Come on," said Salazar, nudging Azarak.

"What? Already? We walked all that way just for you to—?"

"Come on," the young man muttered.

Azarak growled, but nonetheless said good-bye to Azir and motioned for Avamor. The two warauls padded alongside the young man away from the clearing, exchanging glances with one another.

"I suppose it didn't go well, then?" said Avamor.

"Don't tease me," Salazar muttered.

"I wasn't. What happened?"

Salazar just shook his head and kept walking.

Chapter Thirty-Seven

Rhia was reading that afternoon when Asmodeus lumbered into her burrow.

"What in ze world did you do to poor Zalazar?" asked the moranter, settling down on the floor beside her bed.

"What do you mean?" she asked, marking her place and shutting the book. She rolled over onto her belly so to look over the edge of the alcove at him.

"Ah mean ze poor boy looked zhoroughly dizheartened when he left earlier. What did you zay to him? Did you inzult him? Why would you do zhat?"

"I don't think I did," she replied. "I just told him that I'd never been friends with another human and that I didn't know if I wanted to be."

"Rhia!" Asmodeus exclaimed, looking up at her with plaintive eyes. "Why would you zay zhat? You could ztand for a bit of company."

"I have you and all the others."

"Ah mean company of your own kind, mah dear. You won't be able to ztay wizh uz *forever.*"

"Why not?"

Asmodeus sighed and put his head up over the edge of the bed. Rhia stroked his mane, looking at his face expectantly.

"You are a mortal, Rhia," said the moranter. "Az much az Ah want you to be like uz, you are not, and zhere are only a handful of people who can zee zhat you become zhat way. *Zalazar* iz one of zhoze few people."

Rhia looked surprised.

"He zeemz to be a very nize boy," Asmodeus continued. "If he iz anyzhing like hiz fazher, he will be a very good man. You two are ze only hoomanz for *milez.* Ah know you bozh muzt be lonely for your own kind."

Rhia looked away from him, blushing a little.

"He said I was pretty," she said, "And he was looking at me like… I don't know what, but I don't think I liked it."

Asmodeus chuckled, sending a puff of warm air out over her arms.

"And would it be zo bad if he *doez* zhink you are pretty?" he inquired. "Lizten, child: you have very little in zhiz world. Your family iz all Immortal, while you are not, you live in zecret in ze wildernezz in a hole in ze ground, you have no plaze for yourzelf outzide of zheze woodz—"

"I like it here!"

"But it iz not where you are zuppozed to be," said Asmodeus. "Ah love you very much, but hoomanz need ozher hoomanz, juzt like moranterz need ozher moranterz. Hoomanz are meant to live in ze zun, in houzez, among each ozher." He glanced toward her bookshelf. "Ah bring you all zheze ztoriez about adventure and friendzhip and love. Wouldn't you like to tazte it for yourzelf at leazt onze?"

Rhia glanced away, not sure how to answer.

"And let me tell you zomezhing, Rhia," he continued. "Zalazar iz ze zon of a very important man, and zhall one day be an important man himzelf. He can enzure zhat you are taken care of *forever*, could give you anyzhing you want. Would it *really* be zo bad if he likez you?"

Chapter Thirty-Eight

For the next few days, Salazar slogged around the Den like a creek in the dry season. He tried to occupy himself with magic or his studies, but to no avail. Even the news that Seraphious's warauls had been seen roving the forest in greater numbers could not stir him out of his depressed stupor. For all his efforts to distract himself, his mind kept coming back to the question of why Rhia didn't like him.

Salazar had numerous theories. One of the most prominent was that she didn't like his face. He had spent an embarrassing amount of time studying himself in the mirror and decided that while he was not as unnerving as his father (*thank goodness* he'd been spared the red eyes), he was still disconcertingly white with long, pointy features he still had not fully grown into. He looked through Fildahorr's magic books, but found nothing that could alter his appearance, so just resigned himself that he would have to live with it.

His mind concocted other (and more ridiculous) things; perhaps she was one of those mysterious women who were only attracted to other females, or maybe she had a secret desire for moranters, or maybe the reason she'd been abandoned in the woods was because she was the daughter of a demon just waiting to feed on the blood of men and so Salazar was much safer to be away from her. In the end, he decided she was just scared of him, both because he was a murderer and a man, and *that* was a problem he could do something about.

Salazar resolved that he would return to the Moranters' territory to prove himself a worthy suitor. He spent the afternoon practicing his magic, planning out beautiful spells that would surely enchant her. When evening came, he ventured outside into the clearing, heading towards Arra's circle as he often did.

Before he could get there, there was a blinding flash of light and an instant howling from the guards as the Gate opened. The warauls were all on their feet, surrounding the glowing portal in a wary semi-circle. After a moment, a strange creature stepped through the archway.

Salazar gazed at the newcomer in wonder. His body was like a horse, a humble chestnut in hue. Tall leathery wings curved over his back and a scorpion tail hung curving over the leaves behind him. His dragon-like head was golden scaled, a tall leathery frill sweeping back from around his face with a majestic grace. His emerald eyes surveyed the surrounding creatures and paused at Salazar. A smile twitched at the corners of his mouth and then he spoke, the two golden whiskers that hung from either side of his nose bobbing with the words,

"Greetings, Guardians," his voice was deep and strong, "It is good to see you again."

"Ancient Chai Karan," Fildahorr said, "To what do we owe the honor?"

"I have come for many reasons, Guardian," the Ancient replied, "But few I can tell you. I will stay with you only for this night, and I must speak to you on a most important matter."

"Come," said Fildahorr. "Let us go inside."

The crowd parted to allow the Ancient and the Guardian to pass and descend into the Den. Salazar wanted to follow, wanted to speak to the creature, but decided to wait. After a moment, he went inside and down the hall to his room.

He took a seat on the cushion in the floor and pulled a book from the packed shelves nearby. He ran a finger down the table of contents and flipped to the appropriate page.

"The Ancient Time. Temticìl. The Watcher. The Knowing. Chai Karan.

Time is the oldest of the Ancients, created first after the

Beginning. He is thought to be the most powerful of the Ancients; the supremacy of his power is often contested with the Gateway's. Little is known about Chai Karan's abilities as an Ancient. He resides in the valley of the Arayan Mountains as the leader of the Drokamerdors, the species chosen as his physical form. He remains secluded, venturing little into the rest of the kingdom. He gives help to other creatures of Etheria only if they are in dire trouble, another Ancient is involved, or he is instructed to do so by one of the many prophecies known to the Ancients.

While all Ancients are renowned for their wisdom, Chai Karan is perhaps the most knowledgeable. As the incarnation of Time, he possesses great knowledge of the past, present and future, even more so than the rest of the Ancients. He guards his knowledge carefully, reluctant to disclose information even to the High King himself.

Time was not always a reclusive being. In earlier times, he was an active friend to the people. He and the other Ancients helped the First in building the Etherian society and after the Arrival of the others he remained an active member of the kingdom.

It is said that Time once was married to another drokamerdor and was to have a child by her, but she was slain by the Wraiths before Time's child could be born. Consumed by his grief, Chai Karan erased all traces of her, locked himself away in his castle and did not emerge for many months, not even to eat, for food is not necessary to an Ancient's survival. It is said he wanted above all else to die, and that he even tried to slay himself, but Ancients cannot die, not even by their own accord, and so, Chai Karan remained a slave to his grief.

This tragedy would account for the sudden disappearance of the Ancient from his previously public presence. He now rarely leaves the Arayans and speaks to few, remaining in his palace, awaiting the time he will be required by the One to leave his seclusion once more."

Salazar glanced up from the book. If Chai Karan was as much of a recluse as the book said, then there must be something dire afoot to bring him to Earth. Intrigued, the young man set the book aside and went out of his room to creep down the hall towards Fildahorr's door. He stopped just outside of it, turning his head to listen.

"I can't," Fildahorr was saying, "I couldn't bear to tell him I have failed. I will fix this—"

"You have had centuries," came Chai Karan's deep voice. "And still Seraphious roams freely through the Kwynnish Forest. He has attacked the heir of the Somadar, and yet you *still* do not think it time to speak?"

"What would I say? How would I explain that my own kind have betrayed us? That we, who were sworn long ago to defend this Gate now threaten it ourselves? I can contain them, I just need—"

"You cannot, Fildahorr. Seraphious has bided his time til now, slowly stealing your numbers in hopes of simply undermining you and returning to Etheria without bloodshed, but no longer. His followers have grown impatient. Their years in the wild have hardened them. They have hunted the game in their territory almost to extinction; they are starving. They will not wait longer. If they must shed blood to get home, they will do it. They have already proven that they will. Do you *know* just what would have happened had Salazar been killed? Do you have any idea what it would do to the future? That it would have been *your* fault?"

There was no reply from Fildahorr.

"I know how much this hurts you," Chai Karan continued. "I know the price you have paid to be here, to remain here all this time and to have Seraphious betray you. There is no shame in asking for help—"

"But there is shame in failing at the one thing you swore to do."

"You have not failed yet. Do not wait until it is too late. Lask is but a few days ride from here. He is your Protector. Call on him—"

"And what could he do? Could he even get here with Seraphious roaming the woods? What—?"

"If he can find Galator in this place, I don't imagine Seraphious would be any different—"

"How would I even get word to him? I can't very well send a waraul out of the forest to go traversing the mortal countryside."

"Perhaps *Salazar* could be of assistance."

Suddenly, the door swung open by what must have been magic and Salazar was caught standing there.

Fildahorr gave him a look.

"Do come in, young sir," said Chai Karan. "It is much more comfortable in here." His tail pushed one of the cushions toward the young man.

Salazar shuffled inside, looking thoroughly guilty and settled down across from Fildahorr, whose ears were pressed back with his disapproval.

"It is a pleasure to meet you, Salazar," Chai Karan said, holding his golden head high and regarding him through eyes that seemed endless.

"Likewise, great Ancient," Salazar answered.

Chai Karan gave a satisfied rumble.

"I understand you have become proficient in magic," the Ancient said.

Salazar nodded.

"Can you scry?"

"I can."

"Good. Then you will be able to contact your father from here and no one need venture out into the forest alone to carry a message."

"That won't be necessary," said Fildahorr. "I have had patrols searching the forest for Seraphious. We are more than capable of dealing with him on our own."

"No Fildahorr, you are not," Chai Karan growled.

The waraul looked at the Ancient and Salazar could tell he was biting his tongue only because it was Chai

Karan.

"I did not only come this night to persuade you to ask for aid, but also to warn you," continued the Ancient. "You will be attacked this night."

"Why did you not tell us this immediately?" Fildahorr demanded.

"It would make little difference. You would not have gotten to them in time anyway."

"*What—?*"

"One of your patrols. They found him. Or rather, he found *them*."

Fildahorr was instantly on his feet and running out the door, howling an alarm, shouting for Seppish and Avamor.

Salazar hesitated for a moment, glancing to Chai Karan, who was watching him with curious, but cold, eyes. The young man left the Ancient and went running after Fildahorr. He went up into the clearing, which was filled with a cacophony of shouting and barking. The warauls assembled themselves quickly and were running out into the night within minutes. Salazar accompanied them, keeping pace with them for the time being, though he knew they would outrace him in time.

Their howls rang off the trees as they ran, calling for their fellows, but only the inky silence of the night met them. It was so black, Salazar could hardly see, but

Azarak had come up beside him and ran brushing against him, guiding him along through the forest with eyes far keener than the human's.

As he was growing winded, Salazar suddenly felt Azarak's teeth snag on his pant leg, pulling him to a stop as the warauls came to an abrupt halt.

There was a low whine from up ahead. The warauls made their way forward, watching the surrounding forest, ears pricked for any sound of an ambush, but none came. The woods were deathly still and silent, and the ragged whine came again.

Salazar broke from the ranks first as they came to the small clearing, rushing forward to kneel beside the first fallen form. The waraul struggled under his touch, gasping,

"Seraphious! Seraphious—"

"We know," Salazar assured her, smoothing down her rumpled and blood-spattered fur.

Fildahorr had the warauls accompanying him gather branches. Salazar hefted the wounded waraul in his arms to place her on the litter Seppish and Azarak had prepared so she could be carried back to the Den.

More of the wounded littered the clearing further in; at least fifteen shapes lay scattered like pieces of broken glass. Some whined piteously as they heard the approach of their companions, but there were a few that the final silence of death had already settled upon.

Salazar found himself needing to be everywhere at once. He was being called to help the worst of the wounded, yet it seemed that every fallen waraul was as injured as his fellows. The young man did what he could for them, staunching the bleeding however he could, shredding his shirt and the hems of his pants, anything to help get the warauls back to the Den where they could be better treated.

Once they had gathered the entire patrol, Salazar followed the warauls back into the Tress. He entered the Den and went to the room where the wounded lay. The other warauls were already cleaning the wounds of their fellows as best they could. Salazar turned to Avamor, saying,

"Go to my room. Bring my herbs and any other supplies I have."

The waraul obeyed and returned in a moment, carrying Salazar's healing supplies. The young man laid them out for the warauls to use, then pulled his medallion off over his head, going to the corner where Seppish was lying beside a golden brown female, who was gasping, blood spattering her muzzle with each breath from the gashes that raked down her neck and along her side. Seppish shook his head. Salazar, ever stubborn, pushed him out of the way and knelt at her side, bending down to place his hands on her, one hand pressing the medallion against her side.

He bowed his head and golden sparks began to rise from his hands, tumbling down his fingers like leaves blown along on the wind. They poured out from him, scattering across the waraul, sinking into her, and Seppish looked on, amazed, as her wounds knitted themselves back together.

When Salazar withdrew, the waraul lay still, sides rising in the steady rhythm of sleep, marked by healthy scabs where gaping wounds had been before. Seppish looked at him, amazed and grateful.

"Salazar!" barked Azarak.

The young man rose and went to where his friend stood over another waraul, whom Salazar knew as Estynn, who convulsed and coughed, blood flowing from his mouth. The enemy's jaws had closed around his neck; it was a wonder he was not dead already. Again, Salazar knelt and covered the wounds with his hands, the sparks already rising out of him. He stayed bent over the waraul until his shaking subsided and his breath returned to an even rhythm.

No sooner had he finished than Salazar heard his name called again. He worked his way around the room, but each waraul sapped more of his strength until it was all he could do to raise his hands. He knelt there over a brown female, the magic sluggish to answer him. He looked up to see Chai Karan standing there in the doorway.

"Help me," Salazar said.

"I cannot," the Ancient replied.

"What?" the young man said, not understanding. "You are an Ancient. You could heal this whole room with a word—"

"I cannot," Chai Karan said again.

"Cannot or *will not*?" Salazar demanded. He stood up and strode across the room to him, drawing himself up to his full height to so look the drokamerdor squarely in the face. Chai Karan just shifted his long neck, holding his head still higher.

"Please," Salazar begged of him. "You have more power than any of us could imagine. You could save them, all of them—"

"It is not my place."

"Not your—? *What*? You came here! You warned us! How—?"

"I have already done too much. We Ancients are bound to great and terrible laws, sworn directly to the Creator. I cannot—"

"You *can*," Salazar snapped, "But you *won't*."

"I would if—"

"Damn the rules! You could save all of them! It

shouldn't matter if you would be punished for it; you could save so many, surely that is worth—"

"You cannot understand," snarled Chai Karan. "You do not know how much a single life can change everything. I cannot interfere. I cannot and will not risk disrupting the Plan, and certainly not for the sake of an impertinent boy."

"Then you are a coward," Salazar growled back. "A selfish and *arrogant* coward!" He turned to go back to work.

"I will not be spoken to in such a—"

"Then *leave*!" Salazar roared, rounding on him. "Get out! If you will not put yourself to use, then *get out* and stop wasting my valuable time so I can help them."

"You cannot save them all," Chai Karan told him, and there was sadness in his eyes.

"And you will save *none*," Salazar snarled.

Chai Karan regarded him through narrowed emerald eyes, then turned from him to go clopping away through the Den to return through the Gate.

Salazar turned back to his task, pouring out every drop of magic he could summon. He continued around the room, fighting the sheer exhaustion, wringing the magic out of himself, until he knelt by a wheezing female and could hold himself up no more. He almost collapsed on top of her, but managed to catch himself. The medallion dropped to the floor with a metallic clank and the waraul shuddered beneath him, her life flickered out.

Salazar pushed himself away from her, fumbling for the medallion, stiff fingers closing around it, knuckles scraping against the stone as he crawled toward another waraul, but Azarak came, pushing up against his side.

"Salazar," he said, "Enough. You've done all you can."

"No," he gasped, pushing past him, "I can—"

"There is nothing more any of us can do," Fildahorr murmured, standing in front of him.

Salazar looked at him through blurry eyes, shaking on his hands and knees, before he collapsed at the Guardian's feet.

Chapter Thirty-Nine

When dawn came, Salazar awoke with a start. The warauls had dragged him into his own room. Salazar rose and rinsed his hands of the warauls' blood, then wandered the Den like a lost man. Everyone was busy with something; tending the wounded, bringing food or water, collecting information from the survivors who were conscious, organizing new defenses. Three more warauls had died of their wounds in the night, making it a total of eleven dead. Arrangements were being made to take them back through the Gate to be cremated in Etheria. No one noticed the young man as he passed. He looked in on the warauls, some weeping, some snarling with rage, some simply lying down, defeated. Salazar wished desperately for someone to talk to, longed for a steadying human hand on his shoulder.

No one noticed him as he slipped out of the Den,

crossed the clearing, and walked out through the brush wall. His feet carried him westward, faster and faster til he was running through the trees. He carried his sword over his shoulder, not caring that he was alone, daring Seraphious to attack him now. Salazar was sure that he could take off the waraul's head this morning.

He was panting when he slowed down just beyond the Moranters' clearing. He took a moment to catch his breath, then walked on. Most of the moranters were still down in their burrows asleep, though a few had chosen to doze aboveground. There were a few awake, blinking at him with sleepy, curious eyes. Kairn was one of the few awake and he came lumbering up to stand before the young man.

"What are you doing here zo early?" he asked. "Why are you alone?"

"I want to see Rhia." Salazar made to go around him, but Kairn blocked his path.

"Zhe iz not even awake yet. Even if zhe waz—"

"I'm in no mood for you," Salazar snarled, looming over the moranter, no longer afraid of him. "I've been up all night watching warauls die! I've had my hands soaked in blood for most of the night! I need someone, *anyone,* of my own kind to talk to and you are standing between me and the only human for miles. I am not about to let you stop me."

There must have been a fire in his eyes, because Kairn did not make another move to stop him when Salazar barged past him. The moranter turned his head back, looking after him, but Salazar ignored him. He went to the familiar burrow and knelt down, calling,

"Rhia?"

There was no reply. He climbed down into the burrow, the sound of his feet hitting the hardened floor making Rhia stir from her place sleeping in the alcove. She opened her eyes and started at the sight of him, sitting up, drawing the bearskin blanket up around her.

"Salazar!" she exclaimed.

"I'm sorry," he said, "I just…" He looked at her, the way she sat there in her nightgown, watching him with surprised hazel eyes. "Please don't send me away," he said. "You don't even have to talk to me if you don't want to, just let me sit here." He sank down and rested his back against the wall. "I watched eight warauls die last night. I did everything I could to save them, but I couldn't. There was an Ancient there, but he wouldn't help us. He just stood there, looking at me. I used all the magic I knew how, exhausted myself, but it wasn't enough. Fildahorr doesn't know what to do anymore. Everyone's scared and Seraphious is still out there and I never asked to be in the middle of this. I shouldn't have to feel responsible for all of them, but for some reason I do."

He looked up at her and then seemed to realize just where he was.

"I'm sorry," he said. "It's very early. I shouldn't have just barged into your bedroom and woken you up." He caught sight of something on the wall then, one of her charcoal drawings. It was the only human face on her walls other than her own and it was his. Salazar recognized himself instantly and thought that she had been very kind in her depiction.

Rhia said nothing, but slid out of bed and crossed the small chamber to kneel down in front of him. Salazar looked across the space between them and Rhia saw only vulnerable sadness in his face. It was not the face of a predator, of a murderer, only a lost, lonesome creature. She reached out and pushed a stray lock of his dark hair out his face, then shifted in closer to him, wrapping her arms around his neck. Salazar drew her to him, hiding his face in her thick curls. He heard her voice beside his ear,

"I'm sorry, for all of it. I was cruel to you the last time you were here and I shouldn't have been. I haven't been around other humans very much; I'm not very good at it yet. I have missed you and wished that I hadn't made you feel like you couldn't come back." She hugged him tighter. "And I'm sorry for all that has happened to you."

Salazar said nothing, just holding her there against him, thinking that her presence alone was a greater comfort than anything else could have been. He could feel the warmth radiating off of her skin through her nightgown, warming him from the morning chill. There was an earthen, but sweet, smell that clung to her skin and hair. Salazar did not want to let go of her, but he heard heavy footsteps in the passage outside the burrow, and relinquished her when Kairn appeared. To Salazar's surprise, the moranter did not look angry. Asmodeus appeared behind him.

"Zalazar," he said. "What haz happened? Kairn zayz zhat you told him zomezhing haz happened to ze Waraulz?"

Salazar nodded and related the night's events to the pair of moranters. Rhia sat there beside him and kept an arm around his shoulders, for which Salazar was grateful. The moranters were silent, listening to him with intent expressions. When he had finished, Asmodeus said,

"Ah knew Zeraphiouz had dezerted Fildahorr long ago and zhat he had taken a number of waraulz wizh him, zhough Ah had no idea it waz to zhiz extent."

"He is ashamed," Salazar replied. "He thinks he has failed as the Guardian and wants to make it right so that his failure will not have to be made public."

"We could have helped him," said Asmodeus. "We *will* help him. Ah will azzemble mah moranterz and we will come to ze Gate. After lazt night, it zoundz like he could uze ze extra gaurdz."

Salazar nodded, grateful.

Just then, there was a howl from outside.

"Probably looking for me," Salazar muttered.

Asmodeus climbed up to poke his head out of the burrow, looking out across the clearing. Another howl came and the moranter's silver brows drew down over his eyes.

"Kairn," he said, pulling himself up out of the burrow.

Kairn followed him, then turned to put his head back down in the hole, growling,

"Bozh of you, *ztay here*."

Rhia looked from Kairn to Salazar, not knowing what to think.

There were more howls and barks coming in the distance, and the sound of the moranters shuffling through the leaves. One of them hissed. They could hear Asmodeus's voice from across the clearing, but not enough to discern the words. There was silence, and the moranter's voice came again, louder, and Salazar heard him say,

"Zhiz iz not our war! You have no buzinezz here!"

There was a sudden chorus of hisses and snarls, the sound of scuffling and a high yelp. Salazar got to his feet. There was another howl and suddenly there was an entire cacophony of barking and hissing. Salazar peered up into the clearing.

There were warauls everywhere. They flung themselves onto the moranters, snapping and scratching. The moranters met them, their thick claws tearing into the warauls' furry hides. Salazar looked on in horror, knowing it was Seraphious's force.

"We have to get out of here," he said, looking back to Rhia. "Make a run for the Gate, tell Fildahorr."

"Kairn said to—"

"What's to stop them from coming down *here?*" Salazar growled. "Stay behind me." He drew his sword and climbed up out of the burrow. Rhia pulled herself up behind him.

Everywhere there were struggling bodies. Warauls flung themselves onto moranters, the combatants rolling and floundering in the leaves, falling into the burrows, kicking and scratching and snapping. Salazar took Rhia's hand and the two took off running, weaving around holes in the ground and around the battling creatures.

A waraul spotted them and lunged. Salazar pushed Rhia behind him and sliced out with his sword, carving off the snarling head with a swift lucky sweep. Rhia screamed, but Salazar was running again, towing her with him. They reached the trees and continued on. Two warauls came after them and Salazar turned to face them, planting his feet. He swung at one and the waraul yelped, collapsing as the sword blade sliced along his side. The other one's teeth closed around his arm and Salazar kicked at the creature, dislodging him and sending him sprawling. He stabbed the other as he was getting up and whirled to meet the other driving his sword down the creature's open mouth.

Without wasting a moment, he wrenched his blade loose and took off again, ignoring Rhia's horrified face. The two wove through the trees, leaping over fallen branches, stumbling down the steep hills. Rhia kept up with his long stride, her pace quickened by fear.

It was a long way back to the Gate, but the two ran as fast as their legs would carry them. As soon as Salazar knew they were nearing the perimeter of the Tress, he started shouting,

"GUARDIANS! Seraphious is after the Moranters!"

There was an answering howl in the distance and four warauls came running out to meet them.

"Tell Fildahorr!" Salazar exclaimed. "The Moranters are under attack! We have to go!"

Two of the warauls ran on ahead while the others ran alongside Rhia and Salazar as they made it to the clearing. They were both gasping when they reached the Gate and Salazar spied Fildahorr across the clearing, barking out orders. A good number of warauls were already assembling there. As they prepared to leave, Salazar turned to put his hands on Rhia's shoulders.

"Stay here," he told her. "They'll look after you."

"Don't go," Rhia begged, grabbing his arm in a terrified grip.

Fildahorr threw back his head and howled, the assembled warauls charging out of the clearing.

"I have to," replied Salazar. "I will be back." He placed a hand against her face, then stepped back, turning to join the running warauls.

The way back to the Moranters' clearing seemed even longer than before. Salazar could feel his lungs burning as he ran. His legs felt heavy and he fell further behind. Azarak dropped back from the group, jogging alongside him.

"Come on, two legs," said the waraul. "Not much farther."

When they arrived back at the Moranters' clearing it was a horrific display. Blood of both creatures covered the ground, shrieks and yelps rang in the air and Salazar watched as the warauls fell upon their own brothers. He threw himself into the clearing with them, plowing into a waraul that had lodged his claws into Azir's back. Salazar kicked the waraul off of him and staked him to the ground with his sword. Azir scrambled up again, giving a curt nod of thanks before throwing himself back into the fray.

The forest rang with frantic yelping and the harsh shrieks of the moranters. Salazar had a hard time discerning friend from foe among the warauls in the struggle, and so went for the ones that were after the moranters. His sword carved up fur and flesh, spraying blood up into his face. He lost himself in the horror of it, body moving of its own accord, whirling and hacking, taking life and saving it. His mind went blank in the swelling tide of crimson, and he fought out of frantic instinct.

Something plowed into him from behind, tackling him forward to go tumbling down into one of the burrows. He hit the floor below and swung his arm back, cracking his attacker in the head with the pommel. He was rewarded with a high yelp and struggled out from under the waraul, turning to meet him, snarling as much as the creature before him. The two leapt at each other and Salazar flung himself on the waraul, driving his sword down into the creature, pulling it out, stabbing again, even after the waraul was dead.

He brought a hand up, wiping the blood out of his eyes then scrambled up out of the burrow back into the clearing. He saw Kairn nearby, writhing on the ground under three warauls. Salazar flung himself onto them, blade swinging at them like a scythe upon wheat. He reached down, fingers digging into the furry hide of one, hauling the creature off of the moranter, flinging him to ground only to be struck down under the sword.

Salazar swung back for the other two, kicking one away from Kairn's face. The moranter finished the work with his claws while Salazar lunged at the remaining one. The waraul leapt to meet him and the two collapsed out into the leaves kicking and grappling with each other. Salazar stabbed the creature in the side, heaving him off, rolling over to stab his blade into the waraul again. He pushed on the blade, driving it further into the dead waraul. A large, clawed hand closed over his steadying him.

Salazar looked up to see Kairn standing over him, sides heaving with great wheezing breaths. The moranter nodded, slowly, and Salazar let go of the sword, fingers aching from where he'd been clenching it for so long. He sat back, looking up to see the enemy retreating, leaving the other warauls and the moranters standing, tattered, behind them.

Kairn lumbered away, limping, and Salazar heard Fildahorr shouting,

"Those who are relatively uninjured, gather the wounded. We will return for the dead."

Salazar pushed himself up to his feet, taking stock of himself. He was scratched and nicked in places, and there was a bite mark on his left arm, but he had managed to escape with no other wounds. Fildahorr trotted over to him.

"Are you hurt?" he asked.

Salazar showed him his arm, but shook his head, unable to find his voice.

"I'm glad that is the worst of your injuries. We will need your help."

Salazar nodded. Fildahorr left him, calling out further orders.

Salazar picked his way through the battlefield. It was a gruesome mess; most of the creatures he passed were dead, torn and ragged, and most of the wounded were able to get up on their own. He saw a familiar figure lying on her side and he rushed over.

It was Blair. She lay on her side, paws out as though she were running. Her enemy's jaws had fastened around her neck, wrenching the life out of her. Her face was slack, looking peaceful in death as though she were sleeping. Before the grief could fully well up in him, he heard a hoarse voice say,

"Salazar?"

He turned and rushed to the source of the voice. Avamor lay nearby, facing away, trying to turn his head to see behind him. Salazar leapt to his side.

"Salazar," the waraul gasped, "I'm glad you're safe."

"Come on, we'll get you back," Salazar said, reaching

to shift the waraul so he could be carried away, only to hear him let out a piteous whine.

"No," Avamor croaked. "No, leave me. I am dying. My back is broken; even if I survived I would probably never walk again. My lungs are pierced. It is only a matter of time..."

"Don't say that," Salazar whispered.

"I am too far gone," Avamor choked, "Where is Blair? Where is my mate? Is she safe?"

Salazar looked down into his friend's deep brown eyes. He couldn't bear to tell him that Blair lay dead only a few feet behind him.

"Yes," he lied, biting back his sorrow, "She's just fine."

"Good," Avamor whispered, smiling, "That is good..."

The waraul gasped and exhaled a shuddering breath, his eyes closing, never to open again.

Salazar bit back a sob and laid a hand on his friend's furry shoulder. Pulling himself together, he rose, forcing down the grief for later and moved on, searching for the wounded. Each creature he passed was dead, or already being tended to. He came to a waraul who lay in the leaves, deep claw marks down his side. Salazar knelt down beside him.

The waraul gasped.

"Don't speak," said Salazar, "It will make it worse if you try."

He reached down, hefting the waraul up over his shoulder. The creature whined and struggled from the pain, but Salazar held him still, carrying him out of the clearing. He came to walk alongside Asmodeus, who was leaving for the Den also.

"Ah am glad to zee you are well," he said, "Ah cannot zay ze zame for me."

Salazar looked to see a set of claw marks stretching down the moranter's left side.

"Fildahorr and Ah have dezided zhat ze Moranterz will be ztaying in ze Waraulz' Den for a time. We may have to zhare roomz until more space can be made. Fildahorr zaid it would be bezt for a moranter and a waraul to be in each. Alzo, zhere zhould be a wounded creature in a room wizh one who is well zo to care for zhem."

"I'll keep this fellow with me then," Salazar said, indicating the waraul he carried.

"You may have a moranter wizh you too. Ah cannot zay for zure."

"That would be alright," Salazar said. He wanted to ask if Rhia could stay with him, but he knew that Asmodeus and Fildahorr would never consent to it, and probably neither would Rhia.

They made their way back to the Den, their passage slow and sore. Salazar had to stop twice and set the waraul down to let his shoulders rest. He was glad the creature had passed out, as it had obviously been painful for him to be carried. Asmodeus stopped with him each time, resting in the leaves, panting. Blood spattered his nose.

When they reached the Gate, Rhia came running to meet them. Salazar assured her that he was alright and she took his word for it, going to tend to Asmodeus. Salazar entered his room, setting the wounded waraul down on one of the pillows. He treated the wounds as best he could, then rose, making rounds through the halls as he had the night before. He used his magic where he could, and made poultices when he grew too tired to summon the magic any more.

When he had done all he could, he returned to his own room, flopping out onto the bed, exhausted. He brought a hand up to his face, covering his eyes. He smelled of sweat and blood, and his ears rang with the echoes of screaming and howling. So lost in the swimming thoughts of blood and chaos, he did not hear his door open and started when a hand lay upon his arm. He scrambled, only to see Rhia knelt there.

"Sorry," she said. "I didn't mean to scare you."

He was frozen there before her, like a cornered beast, looking lost and stunned. He felt her pull at his hand. Her voice sounded like it came from far away.

"Here. Let me clean this."

He felt hot, stinging water on his arm, and the rag felt rough as it dabbed at the bite mark. He watched her rub the poultice into it and wrap it, feeling as though he were watching her work on someone else. When she had finished, she dipped the rag back into the water, then reached up, cleaning the blood off of his face. Salazar sat there, perfectly still, feeling dazed and empty. It wasn't until Rhia finished, set the rag aside, then cupped his face in her hands that he came back to reality.

He blinked those bright green eyes at her and Rhia thought he looked so helpless in that moment. She'd seen him carve the life out of three snarling warauls earlier, but here he was now in front of her, looking lost. She shifted over to sit next to him, pulling him over to her and kissed his head. Salazar was too distressed at that moment to rejoice in it. She held him there against her, her hand rubbing up and down the length of his back, until she drew away, saying,

"I should check on Asmodeus."

Salazar looked after her as she rose, wanting to call, 'don't go,' but his voice had fled again. Soon after she disappeared, she was replaced by the broad, lumbering form of Kairn.

"Ah will be ztaying wizh you, hooman," the moranter announced, "Zince Azmodeuz iz juzt down ze hall."

Salazar wondered how the day could possibly get worse, thinking that of all the moranters, he had to get stuck with the one who had threatened to kill him.

Kairn went over to flop down on one of the cushions with a deep, growling groan and Salazar noticed the extent of his injuries. There was a bite mark on the moranter's neck and on his left foreleg, four deep claw marks ran down his shoulder and continued over his side. In spite of himself, Salazar felt sorry for the creature.

"I," he said, hesitating, "I can, um…"

"Yez?" Kairn snapped.

"I can put some of this on those if you'd like," Salazar offered, picking up the bowl of leftover poultice.

Kairn sighed and didn't say anything. Salazar got the feeling he wanted to say yes, but was too proud to admit he needed help from a murderous human. Salazar picked up the rag and pail of water and went over to sit beside the creature, glad to have something to do.

Even wounded, Kairn was still intimidating. The moranter watched him through wary amber eyes as he wet the rag and cleaned the wounds. Kairn heaved a shuddering sigh and laid his head down, allowing Salazar to work.

Salazar tried to be as gentle as possible in doing so; not only because he didn't want to hurt the already suffering moranter, but because he didn't want Kairn to jump up and maul him for hurting him. Salazar washed the blood off the creature's tough bumpy skin, then dipped his fingers into the poultice.

For a brief moment he hesitated, then began massaging the medicine into the wounds. Kairn let out a rumbling sigh and clenched his clawed feet.

"Sorry," Salazar murmured.

"No," Kairn hissed, "It iz fine. It ztingz, yet it iz relieving. Hooman handz are zoozhing."

Salazar continued to work the poultice into the creature's injuries. For a few moments, both were silent until Kairn said,

"Ah'm zorry, young hooman. I mizjudged you."

Salazar couldn't quite process what the moranter had just said.

"Zorry for zcaring you too," he continued. "You zaved mah life today. Ah owe you. You are far more like your fazher zhan your uncle and Ah zhould never have zaid ozherwize. Azmodeuz and Rhia zeem to like you, zo Ah zuppoze Ah can too."

"Thank you," Salazar replied, unsure of what to say.

"If Ah may be zo bold az to azk," Kairn said, glancing over, "Why did you kill zhat man in Letiana?"

"I didn't mean to. He had hurt me and threatened my mother several times, and claimed he knew the location of the Gate and how to kill us. I tried to stand up to him, but I didn't know my own strength, and I killed him."

Kairn hummed deep in his throat.

"Rhia said you're Asmodeus's brother," Salazar said, looking for a way to keep the creature talking.

"Yez," Kairn said, "Ah am hiz younger brozher. Have you any ziblingz?"

"No," Salazar said, "I'm an only child."

"Ah zee. Probably for ze bezt."

"How come?"

"Well, zhough Azmodeuz and Ah were an exzeption, often timez brozherz will quarrel over power when zhey are of a bloodline of leaderzhip and grow to rezent each ozher. Juzt look at your fazher and Malachi."

Salazar had never thought about it, and wondered just how deep Lask and Malachi's hatred of each other ran. He sat back, finished with his task and rinsed his hands off in the pail of water.

"Ah will zleep now," Kairn said, shifting to a more comfortable position.

Salazar nodded. He took the pail and the bowls back to the kitchen and then came back to his room. Before going in, however, he decided to go check on Fildahorr, though as he neared the door, he stopped. Asmodeus and Fildahorr spoke from within and the door was open a crack. Curious, Salazar stood still to listen in. It sounded like they were arguing.

"There wasn't a need—"

"Apparently zhere waz! You told uz when Zalazar waz attacked zhat you had it under control. If you had told uz zhat Zeraphiouz had become zhiz hoztile zooner we could have helped you, or at leazt been better prepared! Ah have lozt many good friendz zhiz day—"

"As have I. After Salazar was attacked we began searching for Seraphious again, trying to—"

"You didn't try hard enough," Asmodeus hissed. "If you had zwallowed your pride and azked for help before now, none of zhiz would have happened! Ze Zomadar iz but a few dayz from here. Zend for him, he can help uz—"

"With your Moranters now at the Gate, we will be just—"

Salazar slammed the door open, sending it crashing against the inside wall. Fildahorr and Asmodeus looked up at him, startled.

"Damn your pride, Fildahorr!" Salazar snarled. "The Guardians and the Moranters now both lie in tatters and *still* you will not call for aid! You think you can control Seraphious, but you *can't*. You should have spoken of his mutiny long ago and now you have cost many good creatures their lives. I *will* contact my father tonight and—"

"Salazar, you don't understand, I—"

"Don't talk to me like I'm a child!" Salazar roared. "I have spilled enough blood today to drown you in! I have watched enough of these people, *my* people, die this day! It was Somadar blood that put you here, blood that flows in *my* veins. I may not be my father, but I know well enough when you need to be brought to your senses! How many more need to die before you will see what your pride has cost us?"

Fildahorr stared at him for a moment, silent, then bowed his head.

"You are right," he murmured.

There was a tense silence, then Asmodeus said, quiet,

"Zend for your fazher, Zalazar. Tell him we need him mozt dezperately."

Salazar nodded and turned to go, but Fildahorr said,

"Salazar?"

The young man paused, looking back over his shoulder at the waraul.

"Tell him I am sorry."

Chapter Forty

Lask was sitting at his desk that evening after supper, melting the wax over one of the candles for a seal. He had just poured it on and was holding the seal down when he saw a flicker from the corner of his eye. Thinking he might have imagined it, he set the letter aside, then saw it again.

A tiny gold spark leapt out of the water pitcher on the corner of his desk. Something seemed to glow from inside it. Wary, Lask pulled the pitcher over to him, hands barely touching it, as if he expected it to explode. He looked down into the water. It rippled, light flickering from under the surface. The glow twisted and writhed, forming into a familiar shape.

"Salazar?" he asked of the water, surprised.

"Adar," came his son's voice, "I'm glad I found you."

Lask noticed instantly that Salazar looked exhausted, and saw a few scratches on his face.

"What happened?" he asked, "Are you alright?"

"For now," Salazar replied. "We need you at the Gate, Adar. There is a waraul, Seraphious—"

"The deserter?"

"You know of him?"

"Fildahorr spoke of him long ago and said he had deserted the Guardians. Why?"

"He did more than just desert. They've been fighting for centuries. He's been corrupting Fildahorr's warauls, stealing his numbers. He's got several hundred now. They attacked me first, then some of the waraul patrols, and now the Moranters."

"And *why* has no one told me this before now?" Lask demanded.

"Fildahorr was sure he could handle it." Salazar paused. "He's terribly ashamed, Adar. He thinks he's failed you and broken the promise he made to Lu`corian. He is sorry for keeping it from you til now."

Lask sighed as Salazar was continuing,

"The Moranters are badly wounded, as are the Warauls. Many were killed today. The battle was terrible."

Lask saw that all too familiar shadow over his son's face, the darkness that clouds the countenance of every soldier.

"I am sure you were very brave," he told him. "I will

be there as soon as I can, my son."

Salazar nodded, and the light flickered, fading away until Lask found himself looking once more into clear, empty water. He set the pitcher aside, sitting back in the chair and running a hand through his hair. He got up and went out to find Myranda. She was reading by the fire and knew instantly that something was wrong when he appeared.

"What is it?" she asked.

"We must go to the Gate. The Warauls have been attacked by their rogue and the force he has gathered in secret. Salazar used his magic to contact me. I must go to Etheria and gather my soldiers to help them."

Chapter Forty-One

Salazar lay awake that night, unable to sleep. Even if he had been able to ignore the rumbling snores that reverberated out of Kairn and the wheezes of the waraul in the corner, the young man's mind was too restless to sleep. He lay on his back, staring up at the ceiling, seeing every snarling face that had come snapping at him during the day, every life he had sliced out, every friend that had lay dead in the bloody leaves.

There was the quiet scraping of the door opening and Salazar looked over, surprised to see Rhia slip inside, turning to shut the door behind her.

"You're still awake?" Salazar whispered.

She turned back around, seeming surprised to see him looking at her and confessed,

"Azarak snores very loud. Although, I see it is not much different in here."

Salazar sat up and stood, skirting around Kairn to meet her. He nodded to go back out into the hallway and Rhia obeyed. Salazar led her down the corridor and into the warauls' kitchen. It was empty so late at night and Salazar went to revive the embers of the fire. Rhia came and sat down in front of the hearth, stretching her feet out toward the fire to warm them. Salazar sank down to sit beside her.

"Was Kairn keeping you up?" Rhia inquired.

"Partially. Even if it were quiet, I doubt I would have slept well after today."

Rhia reached over and rubbed a hand over his arm.

"Asmodeus said you were very brave," she told him. "He said you saved several moranters, including Kairn."

"It's all kind of a blur, really," Salazar admitted.

Rhia's eyes trailed over his profile, down his neck and his chest to the gold that glinted there in the firelight.

"What's that?" she asked.

Salazar glanced down, having forgotten the medallion was there, so accustomed he was to its weight. He pulled it off over his head and held it in his hand.

"It was my forefather Lu`corian's," he said. "It helps me channel the magic in my blood."

She looked intrigued, so Salazar shifted to a more comfortable position and looked toward the fire. He reached into the lapping flames with his mind and they flared brighter at his touch. His hand pulled at the air and the fire answered; the tongues of flame separated out, shifting into several pairs of fanning wings, until three fiery butterflies flitted over the rest of the fire, sparks flickering in their wake.

Rhia smiled in delight, watching them with all the astonished glee of a child. She shifted in closer to him for a better view, her head almost on his shoulder, watching his hands work and the way the fire answered him. Salazar couldn't help but smile a bit as well when he glanced over to her, and made the butterflies dance around each other, drifting on the smoke, looping and twirling. He summoned a bit more of the fire and formed it into a large rose of flame and the butterflies congregated around it.

Salazar extended a hand and the flower floated out of the fireplace, still blazing, and Rhia looked wary as it neared his hand. Salazar reached out and pinched the stem between two fingers and the fires went out, leaving in their place the largest, reddest rose Rhia had ever seen. Salazar smiled and offered it to her. She took it, feeling its warmth still radiating under her fingers, and inhaled its scent, a strong, sweet and spicy smell.

She looked up at him and when Salazar looked over, he realized she was only inches away. Rhia looked up at him and Salazar leaned over, closing the gap between them, finding her lips with his own. Rhia was hesitant, lingering there for a moment, then pulling back, blushing in the firelight.

"What are you afraid of?" Salazar whispered.

Rhia looked over at him. The pristine white of his skin had been brushed golden in the glow of the fire and the emerald green of his eyes was warm and inviting.

"I'm not going to hurt you," he promised and she could feel the breath of his whisper on her skin.

Rhia felt his cool fingers on her cheek, trailing along her jaw and down her neck, coaxing her back to him. She did not try to escape him this time, letting him slide in closer to her and leaning forward to meet him. His lips were cool like the rest of him, not cold, but a pleasant sort of contrast to her own skin that felt heated with sudden nerves. She felt his arm slip around her, drawing her in tighter to him.

Salazar was glad that she no longer seemed reluctant, feeling her settle in against him, her hand finding its way to his shoulder. Her grip tightened on him and her kiss became more insistent. When she drew back she looked up at him with a shy, but satisfied, grin. Salazar smiled in return, twining his fingers in her thick curls.

He shifted back to lean against the wall and Rhia joined him there, curling herself up beside him. Salazar put an arm around her and bowed his head into her hair, breathing in her scent.

"I've never been this close to another human before," Rhia murmured. She tucked her head into the crook of his neck. "It's nice."

Chapter Forty-Two

Salazar awoke to the sounds of the warauls moving about the kitchen. He found himself still leaned back against the wall with Rhia asleep, still curled up on him. He rubbed a hand over her shoulder to rouse her and she looked surprised to find herself there. Realizing there were others now in the kitchen, she blushed and shifted away from him.

"I should go check on Asmodeus and Kairn," she said, getting up.

She gave him a slight, guilty sort of smile, and Salazar knew she would find him again later. One of the warauls in the kitchen grinned at him once she had gone. Salazar cleared his throat and got to his feet, unable to keep the smile off his face, despite everything that had happened. He passed Fildahorr in the corridor, who was looking grim.

"There you are," said the waraul. "I had come looking

for you before dawn to rouse you for the funeral, but I did not know where you had gone."

"It's over?"

Fildahorr nodded.

"I'm sorry," said Salazar, reaching down to put a hand on the waraul's head. "I should have been there."

Fildahorr leaned against him with a sigh.

"It was a hard day yesterday," the Guardian replied, "And I am sure the days to come will be just as hard. I cannot begrudge you for wanting a bit of peace."

"What can I do?" Salazar asked of him. "Tell me what you need, I'll do it."

"We just have to make sure the Tress is secured until your father gets here."

Chapter Forty-Three

"Just there," hissed Yvana.

Seraphious crouched beside her and peered through the brush. She had come running to get him and Seraphious wondered what could be so important. As he looked out through the trees beyond, he saw the source of her distress.

A tall, black horse came trotting down the faint path, bearing an unmistakable rider. The man was tall and proud, and behind him came a woman with bright hair.

"The Somadar and his mate," Yvana whispered. "It looks like Fildahorr's pride has finally deserted him."

Seraphious remained silent, watching as the man passed.

"What should we do?" asked Yvana. "We could intercept them before they reach the Tress. If he never got there—"

"No," growled Seraphious. "We may have renounced

Fildahorr, but we still owe a vow to the blood of Lu`corian—"

"We are outcasts, Seraphious!" Yvana snarled. "Traitors. He will show us no mercy. If we do not make our move now and kill them while we have the chance—"

"I will not take the life of one of our lords," Seraphious snapped. "And if you try, I will take yours."

Yvana glared at him, looking to where the two humans were disappearing into the trees.

"Ready the others," Seraphious told her. "He will surely go to Etheria for reinforcements. We must make it through the Gate before he can return."

Chapter Forty-Four

When Lask and Myranda arrived at the Gate, the warauls looked relieved to see them. Fildahorr was there to meet them.

"I am glad you are here, sir. We worried that Seraphious might try to hinder you. I had tried to send patrols out to watch for you and escort you in, but Seraphious found all of them. They were lucky to make it back at all."

"We encountered no trouble," Lask replied.

"We brought you more supplies for the wounded," Myranda said, dismounting and indicating the pack her horse carried. "I'll stay and help you. I'm sure you could use the extra hands."

"We are most grateful, lady," Fildahorr replied.

"I must cross into Etheria as soon as possible," Lask said. "Where is my son?"

"Here, Adar!" Salazar called, running to meet them.

They did not turn down any of the side passages, but rather headed straight toward the tall set of doors at the far end of the hall. There were two guards outside, who saluted, and Lask asked,

"Is the king in?"

"He is, my lord," replied one of the soldiers. "He will be most pleased to see you." She pushed one of the doors open for them.

Lask passed inside and Salazar followed, emerging into a long, high-ceilinged room. Columns ran along either side, carved with leafy vines. Between the columns on the left side stood seven statues on small risers, four men and three women. One of them, the second, resembled Lask, and Salazar suddenly realized why the man looked so familiar. It was Lu`corian, looking as proud in statue-form as he had when his spirit had led Salazar. Along the other side of the chamber were seven more risers hosting other statues, but only two of them were human. The first Salazar recognized as Chai Karan. The next was a unicorn, then a dragon, a fairy, a human man, a cloaked human woman whose face was hidden. The last riser was empty.

There was a tall throne at the far end, but no one sat there. It was mahogany, carved with arches and leaves, and behind it hung three blue tapestries. The central one bore the divided circle of Etheria, the left depicted a gold crown, and the right, an elegant golden fish.

Lask turned to the left and knocked on a door there.

"Come in," came a voice from inside. Lask let himself into the room and Salazar followed him in.

Sitting at a desk in front of a large circular window was a kind looking man, seeming to be in his early or mid forties (though Salazar knew he must be *much* older). He was of average height with a portly belly and bright blue eyes. His hair was dark brown and a slightly greying beard grew on his chin. A simple gold circlet glinted on his head.

"Lask!" the king exclaimed, rising from the desk at the sight of them. He descended the three stairs down to the main floor of the room and swept over to them, clapping his hands on Lask's shoulders. "It's good to see you!" He glanced over. "Good heavens, is that *Salazar*?!"

"It is indeed," Lask replied. He stepped to the side so his son could approach, saying, "Salazar, this is Lavancer, High King of Etheria."

"It is an honor to meet you, sire," Salazar said, bowing his head and accepting the king's outstretched hand.

"Likewise," Lavancer replied, "Though we have met, you were just a few weeks old at the time." The king regarded him with a fond smile, then looked to Lask saying, "He looks like you when you came forward to take your oaths."

Salazar couldn't imagine having to take on his father's power at so young an age.

"What brings you here?" Lavancer inquired, leading them back across the room and up toward the desk. He motioned to the few chairs there and the pair sat down while the king returned to his place behind the desk. Salazar looked out the window behind him, seeing a large, lush garden, and the glimmer of a pond outside.

"There is trouble at the Gate," Lask replied. "You remember Seraphious?"

"Yes. He deserted Fildahorr some time ago, didn't he?"

"Yes. Unbeknownst to us, however, he has been slowing corrupting the Guardians and has now stolen half of Fildahorr's numbers. They attacked the other warauls and the Moranters just a few days ago."

"Oh dear," said Lavancer. "I suppose you've come to gather help for them, then?"

"Yes. I shall marshal what soldiers I can and return to the Tress before nightfall. Seraphious could return at any time—"

There was the sound of the door banging open and Salazar turned to see a man with bright red hair standing in the doorway.

"You *are* here!" the newcomer exclaimed, bounding across the room. "And you didn't even stop to tell me!"

Lask rose as his best friend lunged at him, clapping his arms around him in a fierce bear hug. Lavancer just smiled and shook his head. When Lask managed to free himself, he motioned to his son.

"Salazar, this would be Forge, my general and the one I consider a brother."

Forge looked at the young man, wide-eyed.

"*No,*" he breathed, disbelieving, "They age *that fast* on Earth?"

"Afraid so," Lask replied.

"Damn, brother," Forge said to him with an amazed shake of his head. He extended a hand to Salazar, squashing the young man's fingers in a warm handshake, saying with a grin, "How do you do?"

"It's good that you're here," Lask said.

"Oh I know," Forge replied with a grin.

"*Because,*" Lask continued, "I need you to gather what soldiers you can in the next hour. Assemble them from the castle barracks and call in some of Denmahi's numbers to replace them until they return. We'll be returning to Earth to assist Fildahorr with Seraphious and the rebelling warauls."

"Rebelling?" Forge echoed.

"The Guardians and the Moranters have been attacked and badly wounded," Lask explained. "Seraphious could return at any time."

"Not a moment to lose then," Forge said. "I'll go assemble the soldiers."

Lask gave him an appreciative nod and Forge was gone from the room as quickly as he had appeared, leaving Salazar feeling as though he had witnessed a whirlwind.

"Since you're here, Salazar," said Lavancer, "Perhaps we can speak of something your father and I have been discussing."

Salazar glanced over to his father, wary.

"It is difficult having the Somadar out of the kingdom," Lavancer said, "But we have been developing a very good relationship with the mortal kingdoms, particularly Letiana. Their king, Tephanis, has been very interested in using their contact with Etheria to improve his kingdom. I would like to continue having someone I can trust on Earth to mediate relations between us, but I don't think the Senate will let me keep your father there much longer, even if he *was* willing to stay." The king cast a knowing, but fond, glance over at Lask. "So, the Senate and I were thinking that it might be agreeable if *you* were willing to be our ambassador to Earth."

Salazar glanced over at his father. Lask looked far less pleased about this prospect than Lavancer did, but he kept silent and just nodded. Salazar looked back to the king.

"After all," Lavancer was continuing, "You have Kwynnish blood in your veins, as well as Etherian. You have grown up in the mortal kingdoms so would likely know more about them than any of us would. And while I hope your father will be around to carry that sword for many centuries yet, it would likely be good practice for you in handling larger, kingdom-oriented matters."

Salazar was not sure how to answer. He had always assumed he would be able to return to Etheria with his father, to live there permanently once he was of age. He was not particularly keen on being separated from his homeland for an even longer period of time.

"Of course, you don't have to give me an answer to-day," said the king, "Or even in the near future, but do think about it, won't you?"

"I shall, sire," Salazar replied.

Lask and Salazar parted from Lavancer and went back out into the entrance hall. Salazar thought they would likely go back out to the courtyard, but Lask said,

"It will take some time for the soldiers to prepare. Come, I will show you something while we wait."

They walked the length of the entrance hall and Lask turned down the sixth corridor on the right. He slowed as they walked and Salazar saw the first in a line of portraits stretching down the right side of the corridor. The face there was familiar; snowy white with equally pale hair and those scarlet eyes that made him feel small even in painted form.

"Lu`corian," Salazar said.

"Yes," Lask replied.

"I saw him," Salazar told his father, "Or rather his spirit, I think."

Lask looked over at him.

"I know that probably sounds mad—"

"Not at all," Lask replied. "I have seen him myself several times."

"There was something else with him, a moth—"

"A luna moth," Lask said.

"Yes."

"It has always been with him when his spirit appeared to me. I know not why. Sometimes I only see the moth, but I know he is near."

"He led me to Malachi's house," Salazar told him. "If he had not, those warauls might have killed me."

Lask was silent, and Salazar could tell his father was uneasy about the fact he now owed Malachi his son's life.

Salazar looked back to the man in the painting, thinking that Lu`corian somehow managed to look down his nose at the viewer, while still having an affectionate warmth about his eyes. Lask had wandered further down the corridor to stand before the next portrait and Salazar followed. The man painted there looked very much like

Lu`corian, but his face was softer, quiet, kind.

"Siratrian," Lask said, "Your great-grandfather, an able Somadar, and an exceptional healer. It is recorded that he was of great assistance to the castle infirmary. He also raised the dragon Navar, who would later raise *me*."

Salazar considered Siratrian, thinking that he would have liked him very much. His face was much more inviting than Lu`corian's, having none of the pride or mysterious distance in his expression. Salazar shifted down to the next portrait. There was another pale, white-haired and red-eyed face, but one that was very different from the others. He resembled both Siratrian and Lu`corian, but he was harder and there was no warmth in him. His gaze was sharp and flinty and there was an almost sneering downward turn to his mouth. He held his head high, not simply with aristocratic pride, but with cold, unabashed arrogance. As Salazar studied the painting, it felt like those cold eyes were looking back at him, staring into him, calculating, and just being under their gaze seemed to drain the young man.

"Luke," Lask said. "My father."

Salazar looked from the man in the picture to his own father, wondering how Lask had ever come from such a cold, pitiless man.

"I don't like him," said Salazar. The painting continued to stare back at him; the brushstrokes of his eyes seemed to pierce into the young man, inspecting him, judging him.

"Nor did I," Lask admitted. "I did not know him well, for he rarely took an interest in me at all, favoring my brother far more than me. He was always abusive of his power. It is widely believed that *he* was the reason Vortearigan rose and the kingdom fell into chaos and war."

Salazar believed it, even though he knew very little about his grandfather. The eerie gaze of the painting unnerved him, so he shifted away from it. The contrast between Luke and the man in the next portrait was striking. The next man, while still pale, had black hair that he wore tied in a loose ponytail and bright blue eyes. He wore an exuberant, boyish smile, one that Salazar could not help but smile in return to.

"Aborzen," Lask said. "My uncle. He served as the chief spy under King Sendanten, then later took up the life of an explorer. Alas, he sailed out across the ocean toward the West and never returned. I have no memory of him, as he disappeared not long after I was born."

Salazar was sorry for it, thinking he would have liked his great-uncle. As they continued down the hallway, he knew the next man as well.

"Malachi," he said.

Lask nodded. Salazar looked into the familiar face,

thinking it was true he resembled him. Malachi wore that same crafty smirk that Salazar had seen firsthand.

"May he never cross your path again," Lask said. "In his attempt to poison me, he murdered King Sendanten. Everyone thought he deserved execution for it." He paused. "I could not order it."

Salazar thought he heard a note of shame in his father's voice, but could not study his expression, for Lask had walked on. Salazar stopped to look at the final portrait.

"Hopefully you'll recognize him," Lask remarked with a crooked smile. "Handsome fellow, isn't he?"

Salazar found himself looking at his father and thought it was a very good likeness. He was impressed the artist had somehow even managed to capture a bit of the fire that always seemed to be held in Lask's gaze. His father was dressed all in red and gold and sat with his head held high. The sword rested in his hands across his lap, though there was a sunflower on top of it.

"Someday," Lask said, "Perhaps soon, you will have a portrait here."

Salazar looked to the rest of the empty wall that continued down the corridor, trying to imagine himself hanging there among so many ancient and great men.

Lask led him to the end of the hall to a tall mahogany door. It was carved with the seven-rayed sun of the

Somadar and had swirling iron hinges. Lask produced a key and unlocked the door.

For the hundredth time that day, Salazar found himself amazed. The chamber was just as large as the king's study. There were three tall arches at the other end, soaring over the set of five steps, which led up to where the huge mahogany desk sat. The desk was centered in front of a tall arched window, which was flanked on either side by smaller pointed windows. The room obviously belonged to his father, as it was done in his favorite color: red. A long crimson rug led across the chamber and red tapestries hung along the walls to either side, each stitched with gold in either the seven-pointed sun or the hawk of Lask himself. A line of sweeping text was painted over the archways that read: *Lecer è ì vitarènset Aucre kervaniel el ì mortàntenset kervaniel esè lìborniénìm.*

"What does it say?" Salazar inquired.

Lask replied as he crossed the chamber, his voice echoing off the tall ceiling,

"Let I, in living, serve God, and in dying, serve His children."

Lask had ascended the five stairs and now stood before the desk, looking back at his son, waiting for him to join him. Salazar saw again the man he had seen those years ago in front of the fire; a man much more than just his father.

Salazar walked across the chamber and stood at the

base of the stairs for a moment, then followed them up to stand beside him. Lask smiled and went around to pull the tall chair out from behind the desk, motioning for his son to approach.

"Have a seat," he said.

Salazar went over and hesitated for a moment, then sank into the chair, slowly, as if he expected the seat to bite him. He settled into it, leaning upon the straight back, hands settling on the armrests, and he felt very small sitting there. He looked out across the great chamber, feeling as though he were looking out over the whole world. With a certain sense of irony, he then noticed the enormous map that hung over the door on the opposite wall; a map of the entire kingdom, large enough for most of the places to be read even from the desk. As the door was not centered in the room, lining the longer wall to the right were bookshelves, stretching floor to ceiling, accompanied by a movable ladder so to reach the shelves high above. They were all laden with books, scrolls, and other objects that Salazar could not study from his place at the desk. There were also smaller, narrower bookshelves set into the backs of the two columns that supported the arches over the stairs. They hosted what looked like a number of ledger books, as well as a few volumes that Lask had used so much their leather covers were worn and the titles almost rubbed off the spines.

"Comfortable?" Lask inquired with a grin.

Salazar gave a nervous smile. Lask chuckled and clapped a hand on his shoulder.

"You'll grow into it," he said, "One day."

Chapter Forty-Five

"These minutes pass like hours," Fildahorr groused, pacing the outskirts of the clearing.

"He's not even been gone a half hour yet," Myranda remarked.

"And zurely it will take time for ze zoldierz to ready zhemzelves," Asmodeus added.

"I've got a bad feeling about this," muttered Fildahorr, never ceasing his nervous trotting. "Seraphious's agents patrol the woods, I'm sure you were seen upon your arrival. If Seraphious returns before Lask can get back—"

"I'm not so sure we should try to hinder him," said Myranda.

"What?" Fildahorr snarled. "I am to defend this Gate at all costs—"

"You have maybe fifty warauls left at your call," Myranda said, "And perhaps a hundred moranters, but we'd be lucky if half of them are in fighting shape. Seraphious has two-hundred or more, you said."

"Ah muzt zay, Fildahorr," said Asmodeus, "Zhough Ah am not one to run from a fight, Ah do agree wizh ze lady. Zhere would be no honor in engaging Zeraphiouz wizh zo few and zuch a tattered forze. It would be zuizide—"

"I am bound to defend this Gate," growled Fildahorr, "Just as the rest of my kind are—"

There was pitiful yelp from across the clearing. Azarak had been helping one of the wounded warauls out of the Den for a walk, but the other's wounded leg simply could not support him.

"You have nozhing to defend ze Gate wizh," Asmodeus said. "Look, Guardian. Your companionz are ragged and can hardly ztand anymore. Zeraphiouz haz torn zhem to ze very thezhold of zheir livez. How can you azk zhem to fight knowing you lead zhem zurely to zheir deazh?"

There was a howl from somewhere in the distance and Fildahorr's head swung in the direction of the sound.

"One of yours?" Myranda asked.

Fildahorr stood there, silent, tall ears pricked. The howl came again and his head dropped, teeth bared.

"*No,*" he growled. He whirled back to the clearing, shouting, "Make ready!"

Myranda looked back out toward the forest, hearing more echoing howls ringing through the trees. She glanced over to see Rhia there, watching the woods, wide-eyed, and turned back to where Fildahorr was still calling for his warauls.

"Fildahorr," Myranda insisted, "Seraphious is too many and your numbers are already depleted and battered. Get everyone inside, bar the doors—"

"With all due respect, lady, I'm *not* about to just hand over the Gate to—"

"Zhere iz no point in wazting more livez when we already know we are outnumbered and—"

"We could hold them off until the reinforcements come—"

"We don't know how long zhat's going to take. We could all be dead by zhen," Asmodeus growled.

The howls were drawing nearer and Fildahorr looked over his shoulder to the warauls and moranters limping into ranks, all of whom were looking to him, expectant and afraid. There was a sadness in them, Fildahorr saw, the hopelessness clinging to their every pore.

"There is no shame in living to fight another day," Myranda told him, "Let him pass. Lask is already in Etheria and probably on his way to the Gate as we speak. His soldiers can pursue them there. You are not surrendering, you are simply choosing a better battlefield and fighting force. Whether you let them through the Gate or not proves *nothing*. Whatever promise you are clinging to is not worth sacrificing so many."

"Have zheze pazt dayz taught you nozhing?" asked Asmodeus.

Fildahorr looked back out into the trees and then to Asmodeus. The moranter nodded. Fildahorr's jaw tightened, then he threw his head back over his shoulder, shouting,

"Everyone inside! *NOW*!"

Relief flooded through the tattered ranks and the warauls and the moranters poured back into the Den. Asmodeus and Rhia followed after them and Myranda came behind. She and Kairn heaved at the great door that would close off the entrance.

"Fildahorr!" Myranda called.

"Go," the waraul growled, planting his feet out in the clearing. He looked back to her, "*Go*!"

Kairn gave the door another shove upwards and the way was shut, Myranda sliding the bar into place.

Not a moment later, Seraphious entered the clearing, the rest of his warauls prowling in behind him. They looked to either side, but the clearing was deserted, except for a lone shape that stood there before the Gate. Wary of an ambush, Seraphious glanced around, then trotted in further, calling,

"Well, Fildahorr, have the others finally deserted you too?"

Fildahorr said nothing. Seraphious and the others crossed the clearing and stood before him. Seraphious glanced toward the Den and saw the way was barred.

"Hiding, are they?" he said, "Won't even stand beside you?" He gave a satisfied toss of his head. "I suppose I was right then; you're not nearly as inspiring as you think you are."

"Let us finish this," Fildahorr growled. "Here and now, just the two of us."

Seraphious gave him an incredulous look.

"And miss my chance to see Etheria again?" he said. "I think not." He reached out and touched a paw to the cold green stone, opening the golden portal. He smiled. "This is exactly as I hoped it would be: you watching me return home, knowing you have failed in every way."

Fildahorr lunged at him, but two of Seraphious's companions halted his charge, snapping at his face and kicking him back with their paws. Fildahorr snarled, and with a last smile, Seraphious disappeared into the light, the others close behind him.

Chapter Forty-Six

Once they had left Lask's study, Salazar and his father made their way back out to the courtyard, which was abuzz with soldiers. Lask walked straight down the path the way they had come, and Salazar watched as the people parted around him, like minnows evading a pike. They came to the place where Forge sat astride his grey mare, hollering out orders. One of the stablehands came forward with their horses, and the extra that had been prepare to take back for Myranda. Lask pulled himself up into Theramancer's saddle. Salazar followed suit and turned his horse to where Forge was saying,

"There are a little over two hundred here. The reinforcements should be up from Denmahi in another hour or so."

"Two hundred should suffice," Lask replied. "Combined with the Warauls and Moranters we should make quick work of Seraphious."

They set out from the castle at a brisk pace, riding back into the Carthonian and following the way to the Gate. Salazar found himself studying the soldiers behind them more than their surroundings. He tried to be discreet about it, glancing back over his shoulder now and then, taking quick glimpses of their green uniforms, though a few were in brown, observing the way they traveled in sync, side by side as easily as flying flock of birds. When they neared the arch, Lask pulled Theramancer to an abrupt halt.

"Warauls," Forge said, seeing the tracks that had caused Lask to stop.

"Many," Lask noted. His eyes followed them away into the trees, seeing them head north. "Maresyn," he found the soldier among the ranks, "Ride to Scoarin's lair. If she is there, ask her to come to the Gate to help us follow that trail." He looked back to Forge. "Wait here," he told the general. "I will take a score of soldiers through, see what has happened and be back soon."

Chapter Forty-Seven

When Salazar emerged from the Gate, the first thing he saw was Fildahorr sitting in the clearing before the Gate with his head bowed. There were a few warauls and moranters there as well, looking guilty.

"What happened?" Lask asked of the Guardian.

"Seraphious has gone through," Fildahorr murmured.

"My doing," said Myranda, coming to stand before her husband. "Seraphious came not long after you had left. I did not think it would be wise to hinder him with so few in good fighting shape and not knowing how long it would take you to return."

"Zhould we have fought, zir?" asked Kairn from nearby.

"No," Lask replied. He nodded to Myranda. "You did well. We found his trail near the Gate. We will follow it immediately. Fildahorr, gather several warauls and accompany us. No doubt Seraphious heads for Sayden, and you know it better than anyone."

"We zhall come alzo," Asmodeus announced, "You could uze ze extra clawz, Ah am zure."

Lask nodded. He glanced over to see Salazar exchanging a look with Rhia, who was standing by the Den.

"You may stay if you want," Lask told him.

"No." Salazar shook his head. "I will go." He turned his horse to follow his father, his mother pulling herself into the saddle of the horse they had brought for her.

Lask reopened the Gate and they crossed back into Etheria.

Chapter Forty-Eight

It was not long until Seraphious's trail split and Lask knew the warauls had divided themselves to make tracking them more difficult. They paused for a moment so the commander could divide his soldiers to follow each path.

"Spare their lives, if you can," he told them, "But do not hesitate to take them if they will not spare yours. Capture them, if you can, but do not let them evade you."

The soldiers fanned into the Carthonian Forest, pursuing the warauls like the thunder chasing the lightning. Salazar looked up through the boughs overhead as he caught a familiar sound, and soon saw a golden shape come gliding in. The dragon tucked her wings to land among the trees and Salazar saw the dark shape of Falron circle overhead. She gave a nod to Salazar in greeting, then turned to Lask.

"Seraphious has come through, I'm told," she said.

"Yes," Lask replied. "They have divided themselves and we are pursuing each of the contingents. Would you and Falron help us track them and communicate?"

"Of course. I can set fire to them from above, if you'd like." The dragon gave an eager puff of smoke from her nostrils.

"That won't be necessary," answered Lask with a fond smile at the dragon.

Scoarin gave him a disappointed, but resigned look, then leapt back up through the trees, soaring up to meet Falron and relay the orders. When she had gone, Lask led his group onward into the trees.

Chapter Forty-Nine

"We did what we had to," Seraphious snarled over his shoulder to Yvana who had been protesting. "We couldn't risk staying together, then none of us may have made it."

"So you would turn some of us over to the soldiers so that *you* can get back to Sayden?" growled Verrick.

Seraphious rounded on him, halting their frantic run, and plowed into the dissenter, shoving him over to pin him beneath a heavy paw.

"This was *your* idea," he snarled, "All of you!" He looked around at the other warauls. "You wanted to see Etheria again, no matter the cost. I did as you asked and got us here. And here we are! We are outlaws now, the Protector comes hard on our heels and we will have but a moment to savor the air of Sayden. This is not what I wanted! I wanted it to be bloodless—"

"It was never bloodless!" snapped Yvana. "Manea—"

"A mistake," Seraphious snarled, "And one I have paid for every day. I did great harm to one I considered my brother, both for myself and for you." He paused. "I was a good friend for many years—"

"Yet always jealous," hissed Yvana.

"I never wanted this," Seraphious said, "But you have brought me here—"

"*You* have brought us here," growled Verrick from under his feet.

"At *your* bidding," Seraphious hissed, "You cannot place all of the blame on me. What has been done is done, and we have made ourselves into something that cannot be changed or forgiven. We have chosen our side and we must stand with it—"

"We could ask for mercy—"

"*Cowards*!" Seraphious howled. "All these years you live by hate, and now when you must answer for it you cringe like *dogs*! We have slain our brethren and we must make it so that it was not in vain. We will enter the Cannas Gorge, where the battle may be evened, and there we will make Fildahorr hear us. If we must die, then we will die within his sight, so that he may know it was his doing."

Chapter Fifty

The afternoon gave way to evening, and still the riders chased the warauls. Falron flew in as the sun was sinking low, reporting that Lask and his party were on the trail of Seraphious himself. The dragon said the soldiers had caught two small groups of warauls, around fifteen each, and spoke of their defeat and capture.

Salazar looked to his father as night fell, the velveteen darkness settling over the trees, and expected they would stop, but Lask showed no sign of it. Salazar guessed he knew the forest well enough to walk it blind, though several of the soldiers produced lanterns, which they affixed to their spear poles, holding them aloft to light the way.

It was hard to guess the passage of time in the dark. It felt like they had been riding for hours, but for all Salazar knew, it could have only been minutes. After a time, the trees began to thin out, and they burst forth onto the dark expanse of a plain and the sky exploded with stars overhead, no longer tempered by the obscuring boughs of the forest. Salazar looked up at them, awestruck despite their brisk ride and heavy purpose, letting his eyes wander over the endless glittering lights. The air was clear and crisp and he imagined he could have simply leapt up and floated among the stars.

Lask at last called them to a halt in the darkness near a stream so the horses could drink and rest for a time. While they were paused, Fildahorr asked of Lask,

"May I speak with you, sir?"

"Of course," Lask replied and walked away from the group so they could have some privacy. Fildahorr walked at his side, head bowed toward the ground.

"I have done a terrible thing, sir," he said as they came to a stop out under the stars, "I know well that you have every right to take back what Lu`corian once gave me." He brought a paw up and shifted the cord from around his neck, letting the silver medallion drop at Lask's feet. "But I ask that you know, sir, I only did what I thought was right to keep the promise I made to him. Perhaps I was too devoted, too rigid in my interpretation, and too harsh to my fellows. And perhaps, too, my own pride kept me from doing what needed done. I fear I have learned this all too late and that I have been the ruin of my race."

Lask reached down and picked up the medallion, considering it there in his hand.

"The Warauls are few now," he said, "After these battles, you will be lucky to still number three hundred, and of those, over half will be counted as traitors."

"What will become of the others, sir?" asked Fildahorr. "I feel I must take some measure of responsibility for them. Seraphious is a traitor, yes, but I believe most of his followers never meant for things to become as dark as they are. Perhaps in time they could rejoin the guardians' ranks."

"They will be tried for treason before the Senate," Lask answered. "If you wish to make a plea on their behalf, I am sure it could be arranged for you to do so. I do not know what the Senate will ultimately decide, but your rebels face imprisonment, centuries of servitude, perhaps even exile or death depending on their individual crimes."

"And myself, sir?" Fildahorr inquired. "I fear I am as guilty as they are." He put his head down again and said, "I wish to change things, sir, if you see fit to give me the chance. Seraphious was right about a number of things. Perhaps in taking my oath too seriously, I did become something Lu`corian never intended. There was never such a hierarchy in our race while we were in Sayden. I would like to see us return to that state. If you see fit to leave me as the Guardian, I will no more count myself their king, but only their caretaker. I will not try to deny them what they love, nor command them as though I am more than I am." He looked up to Lask's face in the darkness. "There is no noble blood in me and I have proven I am not fit to bear it even if there were."

Lask considered him, turning the medallion over in his hand.

"I will place this back around your neck," he told the waraul, "But when I do, you must take the words you have spoken tonight as your new vow. Defend the Gate and defend Etheria, but do so with the knowledge that you are but a servant to me and to your race. You wear this as the mark of your pledge, not a mark of privilege. To bear such a promise demands a life of service, not a life of pride."

Fildahorr bowed his head and Lask placed the cord of the medallion over his head, so that it hung around his neck once more.

"You are most merciful, Somadar," said the waraul. "I shall not fail you again."

Chapter Fifty-One

The plain stretched on and on in rolling hills, into the night, rocks beginning to jut up out of the ground, making it more difficult to follow the warauls' trail. Scoarin returned frequently, helping to keep them on course, reporting that several more of the waraul groups had been caught and subdued, while others were circling around heading into the heart of Sayden.

"Heading for Tansfarac, no doubt," said Fildahorr. "The standing stones there were our oldest meeting place."

The stars drifted overhead and Salazar soon saw a pale glimmer in the east, as the sun returned, fading the stars away among brightening rosy hues. As the sun rose, Salazar could see the rolling, rocky land stretching out before them and the tall spires of mountains piercing up from the horizon far in the distance. Scoarin came soaring in through the reddening sky, calling down to them,

"Seraphious has not stopped at Tansfarac, he's continued north and descended into the Cannas Gorge. The last of his warauls are joining him there. It is too narrow for Falron and me to enter."

"And too steep for horses," Lask said. "He has chosen his battlefield well. How many are with him?"

"Fewer than a hundred, though it is hard to tell."

"Where is Forge?"

"West of here," the dragon replied.

"Have him gather the soldiers that are farther to the west. Tell them to enter the gorge from the northwest. Tell the soldiers east of here to meet me at the southeast end of the gorge. We will catch them between us."

Scoarin nodded and pushed herself back up into the sky, the wind of her departure buffeting the humans below.

"The dawn speaks of blood," said Fildahorr, "And a war has come to Sayden. Was it only my fault?" he asked, as if of the hills before him, "I have longed to see this place again, but never like this. In our days here, we never dreamed that we would spill each other's blood. I lived only to keep my promise, but in doing so, have I broken it?"

Seppish nudged him, not knowing what to say, but hating to see his friend suffer.

When daylight had banished the lingering shadows from the hills, Salazar caught sight of a long dark line in the distance. As they neared it, he knew it had to be the gorge. Deep shadows still clung to its depths, the sides of the canyon almost perpendicular to the ground. There were about fifty soldiers already there awaiting them. When they arrived, Lask dismounted, looking out over the hills, waiting for the rest his soldiers to appear. As the last search parties came into view, Scoarin came swooping in from above.

"Forge is in position to the northwest," she reported, "Awaiting your order to enter the gorge."

"Good. Tell him to set out, then. We will make our way down as well. You and Falron keep watch from above. Do not let any warauls out of the canyon unless they are accompanied by soldiers."

"Falron and I could easily take a perch on the ledge and set fire to the canyon below. They'd have nowhere to run."

Lask just cast a glance up at her.

"Oh alright," Scoarin muttered, "If you *insist* on being merciful…"

With a strong push from her back legs, the dragon leapt back into the sky, catching an updraft to soar back to Forge's position. Fildahorr stood there, watching her go, his claws digging into the ground.

"Our goal is to force their surrender," Lask told his soldiers. "Wound and incapacitate them, but as before, try to spare their lives if you can."

"Sir," said Fildahorr, "I know you mean to try them before the Senate, which is well and fair, but the penalty for murder and inciting such a rebellion is surely death. Allow me to deal Seraphious that justice myself."

"If you can catch him, you may take your revenge," Lask replied, "For I know well you have much to settle with him."

Fildahorr growled and looked to the soldiers.

"Seraphious is mine," he said, "I ask you do not take this from me."

With that he threw back his head and let out a howl, bounding toward the gorge with a determined stride. Lask and his soldiers followed, leaving their horses out on the field, and beginning the descent into the canyon. Salazar walked at his father's side, picking his way down the rocky slope. It was steep and treacherous, but not impassable. Lask held him back and went first, choosing their path downward and Salazar stepped in his father's footsteps, navigating the rocky climb.

The grit shifted under his foot and the young man stumbled, but Myranda grabbed the back of his shirt, holding him steady. Salazar gave her a grateful smile.

A faint cloud of dust swirled out from under Lask's

boots as he leapt down onto the flat bottom of the gorge. He reached up, offering a hand to help his son down, but Salazar leapt to the bottom as he had, flashing a satisfied grin. Lask just shook his head, reaching up to help Myranda down, although she too ignored his hand and leapt down on her own.

When everyone had assembled in the bottom, they set out, following the narrow, twisting corridor of the canyon. Fildahorr and Seppish trotted out ahead, leading the way. They traveled at a cautious pace, expecting to encounter Seraphious's warauls at every turn, but they were nowhere to be found. The canyon wound on and on.

"This is all my doing," Fildahorr whispered to Seppish. "If I had listened, if I just let them go home when they asked—"

"It's too late for any of that," Seppish replied. "We all made the choice to leave. If they did not have the strength to keep that promise, it is no fault of yours."

The sound of a din echoed out of the canyon from up ahead.

"Looks like Forge found them first," Myranda remarked.

They quickened their pace and it wasn't long before Seppish let out a sharp bark.

Warauls came scrambling through the gorge up ahead, fleeing Forge and the soldiers that were hard on their heels, only to come to an abrupt halt as they came face to face with Lask and the soldiers behind him.

"FORWARD!" came Seraphious's irate roar.

The warauls charged on, and a mass of bristling fur and snapping teeth plowed into the soldiers before them. They were met with cold steel. Salazar could hardly get a swing out at them, as Lask was right there beside him, slicing down anything that came near them. Myranda was there at the young man's other side, cracking the enemy with her spear pole and skewering any that got too close. For a moment, Salazar just looked at them, hardly recognizing the warm, mild parents that had raised him. Myranda looked vicious, red hair wild, body twisting, drawing the enemy's blood at every turn. Lask was an altogether terrifying vision, eyes blazing, the blood of his enemies spattering his pale face like war paint. He plowed ahead into the enemy masses and the warauls cowered from him, like the grain bowing under a tempest. The soldiers followed behind him, crushing any resistance they met.

Lask paused in the chaos, realizing that few of the warauls now fought him, instead lying down prone before them, weeping tears of shame and desperation into the dust.

"Halt!" he called to his soldiers.

Seraphious appeared then, leaping up onto a boulder

to the side.

"Up!" he roared to his followers, "Fight!"

But the warauls did not rise.

"Guardian," wept one, turning beseeching eyes up to Fildahorr, "We have betrayed you. We let ourselves be misled. What began as homesickness has become selfish pride."

"Do what you will to us," said another, "But please, just keep us in this world. If we must die, let it be in our home."

"Stop your groveling!" snarled Seraphious. "This is what you have wanted for centuries! This is what you asked me to lead you to! There is—"

The dark shape of Fildahorr went leaping up toward the boulder, cutting off Seraphious's growl, tackling him off his perch into the dust. Seraphious's powerful back legs kicked Fildahorr off of him, but the Guardian threw himself back at his enemy. Seraphious dodged to the side. The two circled each other, heads low, ears flattened, fur bristling, snarling with dangerous teeth.

"We all wanted what you did, Seraphious," growled Fildahorr, "But not at the price you were willing to pay."

Seraphious lunged forward. He snapped at Fildahorr's head, clawing at his sides and Fildahorr snapped out in return.

"None of this would have happened if you hadn't

tried to be so noble," Seraphious snarled.

"Nor would it have happened if you had been a little more so!" snapped Fildahorr leaping for him.

Their yelps and barks echoed off the canyon walls as the two struggled, grappling with one another, clawing and biting, throwing each other to the ground. Dust smeared in their coats as they rolled. Teeth gouged up tufts of fur, claws drew blood, teeth pierced skin and nicked ears. Fildahorr was more agile, but Seraphious had the advantage of size. He kicked out with his back feet, sending Fildahorr sprawling, crashing back into the boulder. The Guardian collapsed into the dust, gasping. Seraphious leapt for him, teeth aimed to close around his throat.

Lask made a grab for his son, but Salazar had already thrown himself out from the bystanders. The young man plowed into the charging waraul, crashing to the ground with him. The two fell in a heap and Seraphious struggled under him, kicking and thrashing, fighting himself loose. Salazar stabbed into the waraul's side with his knife and Seraphious yelped, twisting away on reflex. He whirled back, snapping out at the young man's face, but before he could reach him, another pale hand locked onto the scruff of his neck jerking him backward, and Seraphious found himself looking up into the vengeful face of Lask. Before the sword blade could be brought down upon his head,

Fildahorr came lunging back.

The Guardian's jaws clamped around Seraphious's throat, wrenching him out of Lask's grip and driving him to the ground. Seraphious gasped and sputtered, kicking at the Guardian who held him down, but Fildahorr clung on, his teeth fastened in Seraphious's windpipe, salty blood bursting into his mouth.

Seraphious struggled beneath him, writhing, clawing at Fildahorr's shoulders, choking for breath. His thrashing subsided, losing strength, and he looked up out of the gorge to the skies of Sayden far above, seeing them fade away as the darkness crept into the corners of his vision. His gasps quieted until at last he fell out before Fildahorr, still and slain.

Fildahorr released him, muzzle stained crimson, and tilted his head back, letting out a mournful, but triumphant, howl. Seppish and the other warauls that had accompanied him joined in, their cries echoing up out of the gorge and across the hills of Sayden.

Chapter Fifty-Two

The soldiers escorted the surrendered warauls to the castle to be locked away in the dungeon until the Senate could decide their fate. Seppish, Asmodeus, and Kairn, remained in Sayden for a time, keeping watch while Lask and Myranda treated Fildahorr's wounds before they made their way back to the Carthonian.

They stopped for the night in the shelter of the great trees. Asmodeus lumbered away to find wood for a fire. He was gone a long time and Salazar realized firewood was likely hard to come by, as the trees were as immortal as everything else. When the moranter returned, he carried with him several long branches that had fallen and dried. When they were broken, it was enough for a modest fire. Seppish caught them a family of fat rabbits for supper and when they had eaten, they settled down to rest for the night.

Salazar laid on his back on his cloak, and the grass was as thick and soft as a comfortable mattress. He looked up at the branches of the trees that towered high above them, and at the stars that flickered through the leaves as the wind blew. He breathed deep of the fragrant night air and could not fall asleep. He knew it would likely be a while before he walked in this world again and he tried to soak in as much of it as he could.

When it was very late in the night, he turned his head to look at his father, who lay still and quiet on his back nearby. Myranda was asleep against his side. Salazar watched him for a moment, studying his profile against the backdrop of the brooding fire. He had such sharp and elegant features; Salazar wondered if he would grow into them as well. His father's skin had taken on the gold hue of the fire and from this angle, Salazar thought it looked as if the lingering flames rose out of him. After a time, he whispered,

"Adar?"

"Yes?" came the answer, quiet so as to not wake Myranda. Salazar was surprised he was awake, for he had looked sound asleep. He wondered if perhaps all fathers could awake so suddenly at the sound of their children's voices.

"Do you want me to be the ambassador after you?"

Lask was silent. After a moment, Salazar saw his eyes

open and gaze up into the trees.

"That is not for me to decide," Lask replied after a moment.

"That wasn't my question."

Lask glanced at him. Salazar studied his eyes; they were Lu`corian's.

"I do not believe good will come of our relations with Earth."

Salazar's eyes drifted to his mother, who was still asleep, and thought of himself, and of Rhia, wondering how his father defined *good*. Lask was continuing,

"I believe in the end such an endeavor will only end in bitterness and grief. How long it will take to reach that end, I do not know, but I believe it will come; perhaps not in my time there, nor perhaps even in yours, but it will come. One day they will hate us for what we are and what we have and what they never will. When that day comes, you and I— if we still live— shall have much to dread. Until then, we can only do what the King and the Senate ask of us."

"Can't we tell him otherwise? Can't we say no?"

"I have spoken my thoughts on this matter before the Senate many times. The majority of them do not agree with me. They believe that if we were not meant to be in contact with Earth, the First and the Ancients would not have built the Gate. This may be true, but I do not believe our forefathers could know all that would come of it, and I believe they may have underestimated the times we have inherited, for we walk now in a far wilder country and savage time."

Salazar was quiet.

"You can say no," Lask told him, voice hushed, "But if you do, you must be prepared to live with the consequences. The Senate will not look kindly on it, and the King will be disappointed in you. They will likely appoint someone else to do it, and you must ask yourself, my son, would you trust anyone but yourself with that duty?"

"And your sword?" Salazar inquired. "Could I say no to that?"

Lask watched him through the darkness for a moment before answering,

"Yes. There have been Somadàrsath who have refused it."

The two looked at each other in silence and Salazar knew they both thought of Malachi, who had refused the blade long ago. His denial of it was likely the only reason Lask carried it now. They both knew there was no one else to take it next but Salazar.

"But I can't refuse it," he said.

"No," Lask answered, "No more than I could."

Salazar looked back up into the trees, feeling as if some great weight sat on his chest.

"But you have plenty of time," Lask told him. "With any luck, I shall live to carry this blade for many more years, likely many centuries yet. You need not fret yourself so right now."

Salazar turned his eyes back to his father. Lask watched him with a quiet, gentle smile, and the young man thought he looked every bit like a father and nothing like the Somadar in that moment.

"And in the meantime?" asked Salazar.

"You must do whatever you feel in your heart to be best and serve your kingdom as you are commanded."

"So I will go back to Earth, and I will walk between the worlds as long as I can." It was not a question.

"Yes," Lask replied, "And I imagine you will do it as well as I, or any man, could."

They fell silent and the night passed. Salazar slept fitfully, dreaming of trees and blood, but he did not remember them when he woke.

In the morning, they made the final trek back to the Gate, where Salazar reached out and touched a hand to the green stone, opening the golden portal. He looked back over his shoulder at the trees and the sapphire sky high above. Lask smiled, knowing his hesitation.

"You'll be back," he promised.

When Salazar emerged on the other side, Rhia was there waiting for him. She threw her arms around his neck when he appeared and, not caring they were in the sight of many, grabbed his head to kiss him.

"I've been so worried about you!" she exclaimed, refusing to let him go.

Lask glanced over at the two of them and Salazar flashed him a sheepish grin. Lask just smiled and turned, walking away alongside Fildahorr, Guardian of the Tress. Salazar put an arm around Rhia and looked back to Gate. It stood proud and patient, full of promise.